DREAM▲WALKER

BOOK ONE

ENTER THE SANDMAN

G.W. Mullins

LIGHT OF THE MOON PUBLISHING

ISBN: 978-1-7377100-1-1

First Printing

This is a work of fiction. Names, characters, businesses, places, events and incidents are either the products of the author's imagination or used in a fictitious manner. Any resemblance to actual persons, living or dead, or actual events is purely coincidental.

Light Of The Moon Publishing has allowed this work to remain exactly as the author intended, verbatim, without editorial input.

Printed in the United States of America

For further information, on his writing, visit G.W. Mullins' web site at http://gwmullins.wix.com/books

Also Available from G.W. Mullins in Hardback, Paperback and eBook

Rise Of The Snow Queen
Book Two:
The War Of The Witches

What begins as a simple, bittersweet tale about a man turned into a polar bear, grandly unfolds into a rich, mythical adventure in the best-selling book series Rise Of The Snow Queen. Based on Hans Christian Andersen's fairy tale, author G.W. Mullins expands on this story creating a new mythology that takes readers into the world of snow and ice.

In part two, the story develops long before the adventures of Gerda and Kai. It takes readers to a remote mountain village where winter claims lives at the Snow Queen's command. The story goes back to the Mirror and how it cracked, sending its shards into the world to infect the innocent. This take on the story, embarks on a much more adult tone with the mood turning rather sinister as the Snow Queen battles to obtain the mirror and rule them all. Rise Of The Snow Queen Two - War Of The Witches, is a dark fairy tale that unfolds to a conclusion you won't expect to see coming.

Rise Of The Snow Queen Book One: The Polar Bear King

The first book from the new "Rise Of The Snow Queen" four part series.

G.W. Mullins has taken timeless folklore and crafted it into a new book series meant for adults. His updated take on the Polar Bear King and Snow Queen pay homage to the stories we all loved as children while making them more adventurous and not always allowing for a "happily ever after" ending.

The newly crowned King Valeman refuses to marry an evil witch, who reveals herself to be the infamous Snow Queen. His refusal to align himself with the dark forces causes her to cast an enchantment upon him.

Her unbreakable spell changes him beyond belief. "By light one way, by night another. Your form will change you will soon discover. By day a beast of a bear you will be, at night a man while others sleep. To break this spell you much achieve, the love of another while being a beast."

Valeman is transformed into the Polar Bear King and given seven years to find true love or the enchantment will be permanent.

***Daniel Awakens
A Ghost Story
Begins***

***Death Is Only
The Beginning***

Author G.W.
Mullins turns
back time in his
Best-Selling
"From The Dead
Of Night" book
series.

In Daniel
Awakens A Ghost
Story Begins, Mullins takes you back to the day
Daniel died. In a welcome addition to the fan
favorite series, readers will learn what happened to
Daniel.

Daniel had known his whole life something was not
right. He never connected with the woman who he
was told was his mother. As his sixteenth birthday
approached, he learned the life he had lived was
based around a hidden past. His worst suspicions
were realized when the truth of his father's affair
came to light. As Daniel ran from the house of lies,
he had no idea his young life was about to end.

Daniel awakened in the cemetery, and quickly came to learn death is only the beginning. Thrust into a world of the undead, he had no time to learn of the afterlife or the battle of good and evil. The dark ones were coming, whether he was ready or not, he would soon learn of the dark-lighters and a force of evil named Malachi.

Destined to be a leader in the fight for the balance of power, Daniel is thrust into a battle he is not ready for. He quickly learns of his abilities and the lack of experience he has to control them. Daniel must fight to save the force of good.

Daniel's Fate
A Ghost Story
Ends
"From the Dead
Of Night" Book
Four

Daniel walked
in the land of
the Dead. Now
the Dead want
him back.

As the dark ones came for Daniel, he was forced to take refuge in the light, the last place he wanted to be. There, he was to decide his own fate. Staying in the light and ascending meant

Jen would be left defenseless. If he chose being human again, the dark ones would have the

power to take over the world. As Daniel made his decision, the dead began to rise. The dark

ones were coming forward to block the light and create hell on earth.

Death is only the beginning... From The Dead Of Night Book 4

***Daniel Is Waiting
A Ghost Story
"From the Dead
Of Night" Book
One***

***Daniel walked in
the land of the
dead. Now the
dead want him
back!***

The veil is lifted
between the
living and the
dead as the
Shadows come
forward to capture him.

Daniel Stratton died in a tragic accident. His life
should have been over but it was not. His spirit spent
the next sixty years trying to communicate with the
people who came to the cemetery where he was
entombed. Then Jen came one night to the
mausoleum seeking refuge from a life that was
spinning out of control. There she found Daniel.

As they work together to free him from his forced
confinement; they learn that the Light comes for all
dead, and Daniel is forced to enter it. In his case there

is no matter of choice. Inside he fights for his life and escapes but the enforcers of the light come for him. He saw seven of these shadow people within the light and each marked him. Daniel knows these Shadows will come for him. Each one of the seven will take the body of a human who had just succumbed to death turning them to Zombie like creatures to do their bidding.

Together Daniel and Jen must confront the "Shadows" so that they can survive to see another day.

Daniel Returns A Ghost Story "From The Dead Of Night" Book Two

Daniel walked in the land of the dead. Now the dead want him back!

The story continues where

"Daniel Is Waiting A Ghost Story" ended in a cliff hanger.

Daniel died a tragic death and should be dead. He walked in the land of the dead for too long. Then the light came for him but he refused it. He fought to escape it, but higher powers had other plans for him.

His fate was to ascend and take on the role of angel, but something went wrong. Before he could assume his role, he met Jen. When Daniel fought the light to stay with Jen, he broke the law of the dead. Within the light seven Shadow enforcers saw him. They reached out to stop him and in doing so marked him. When Daniel escaped, he knew the seven would come for him.

The forces of good and evil watch to see who can claim Daniel in the end and control the ultimate power that is growing within him.

Messages From The Other Side Stories of the Dead, Their Communication, and Unfinished Business

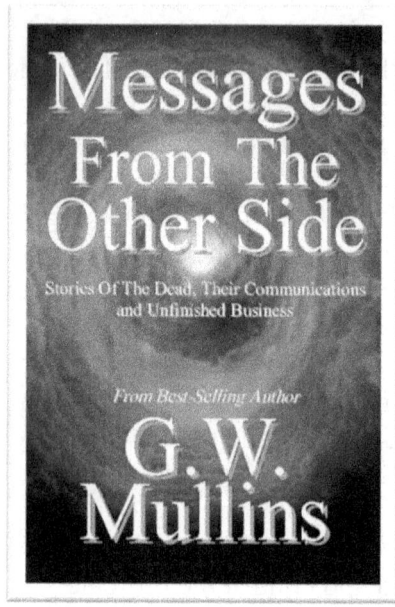

Best-selling author G.W. Mullins shares his personal journey towards understanding death, the afterlife and communication with spirits of loved ones who have passed over. In "Messages From The Other Side Stories of the Dead, Their Communication, and Unfinished Business," Mullins tells of dealing with the grief of his mother passing and the reassurance of an after death communication that totally changed his outlook towards death and grief.

This book not only tells of Mullins' personal journey into understanding but also guides others to understand why we receive communications and the signs to look for. Mullins also explores visitation dreams and tells of his own personal experience in the area and shares the stories of others who have had similar experiences.

This book highlights the author's personal journey in an exploration for knowledge, and his understanding, without question, there is life after death. Mullins invites you to join him on this journey through life and death.

***Vengeance
A Paranormal
Murder Mystery***

*"Mystery,
Murder,
Paranormal
Events, and a
story that leaves
you guessing as
the bodies stack
up."
– Matthew Trent
OutLoud
Magazine*

After the death of her father, Danni starts a new life in a seaside town in New York where she and her mother move into a strange Gothic house with a terrible history. From the moment Danni gets there, she feels she is being watched. She is sure they are not alone in the house.

As Danni learns of her new home, she is told of a past resident who fell to her death on the nearby cliffs at the same time that her teenaged daughter, Elizabeth, disappeared.

Elizabeth's spirit, appears to Danni and claims that her mother's death was a murder, not suicide and asks for Danni's help in bringing the dangerous killer to justice.

The mystery unfolds as Danni enlists the help of the hunky new friend she has made named Joe. A romance develops between them, but does Joe know more about the murder and disappearance than he is letting on? Will Danni live to solve the murder?

Other titles available from G.W. Mullins include:

Timeless - An Adult Paranormal Romance Novel

The Native American Story Book Volume 1-5-
Stories Of The American Indians For Children

Walking With Spirits Volumes 1-6 Native American
Myths, Legends, And Folklore

The Native American Cookbook

Star People, Sky Gods And Other Tales of The
Native American Indians

Cherokee A Collection of American Indian Legends,
Stories And Fables

**Included at the end of this book, are the first two
chapters of G.W. Mullins' Best-Selling title
Rise Of The Dark Lighter Book One –
Dark Awakening**

For Clarence

"A dream is a wish your heart makes, when you're fast asleep."

- Walt Disney

"They've promised that dreams can come true - but forgot to mention that nightmares are dreams, too."

- Oscar Wilde

Mullins

Before

Zach's eyes opened wide as he tried to convince himself he was still awake. He clung to the rock cliff, as his body was thrashed back and forth in the wind. This could not be real, he thought to himself, over and over again as hail and rain felted his skin.

"Someone, help me!" he screamed hoping someone was there.

"Take my hand if you want to live." A voice came from behind him as a blue light filled the area just above his head.

"Who are you? What is happening?" Zach screamed out.

As a hand took his, from the rock above Zach looked up to see his savior. As his eyes moved up, he saw the blond-haired boy grabbing onto him, while holding tight to a rock formation above. As

Zach was helped to climb up, he looked around at all that surrounded him.

"What is this place?" Zach asked.

"You are in the Dream Land. I am Daniel." He responded.

"I don't understand. How did I get here?"

"You really don't know, do you?" Daniel said turning his head away. "This is a realm outside of reality. It is harsh and deadly. Only the strong survive here. I am betting you did not come here of your own free will."

"How do I go home? I don't want to be here." Zach tried to speak, as his body began to shake from the cold air blasts that kept pummeling his body.

"This is the hard part; you are here because of a Sandman. Only your consciousness exists here. Your body is wherever you were, when you went to sleep." He didn't know how else to explain it.

"I thought the Sandman was a fairy tale creature. You can't mean they are real. Daniel please. You have to know a way back." Zach pleaded with him.

"Come, there is shelter above." Daniel turned to walk away hiding the grim expression on his face. He knew all too well, the horrors that inhabited the Dream Land. If the realm or its inhabitants did not want Zach to leave, it would not happen.

As they entered the cave, the roar of the outside died down and the winds disappeared. This place was safe, at least safer than outside. Before them on the ground, was a fire that lit the cave and provided warm. Daniel extended his hand as to offer Zach a seat.

"For a moment we will be safe here. Unless the observers locate us. I have been lucky here since I arrived. It seems this place is beyond their scope. This and the temple that lies far below."

"Why would someone bring me here?" Zach yelled out. "I have done nothing to anyone. Why did this Sandman take me? Better yet, can I get back to my body. What will happen as time passes. Will I die?"

"No, you will not die. Your body will be in a sort of coma, waiting for you. You will age and grow as a boy would, as he turns into a man. I would guess you are around twenty years old?" Daniel asked.

"Yes, how did you know that?" He asked.

"I am good with reading people. Just like I know you have led a pretty sheltered existence. You have stayed close to home your whole life, haven't you?

"Yes, I have always lived with my parents in Big Eden."

"It shows, you went into fear mode as soon as you saw the place."

"I was hanging from a cliff and being beaten by flying objects. Anyone would be scared. How long have you been here?' Zach asked.

"I have traveled in and out of the realm many times over the years. And before you ask, I cannot lead you out of here. If this place does not want you to go, you will not leave. Just try to stay calm and if you are meant to leave, you will…in time." Daniel said coldly as if not to give him any hope.

Mullins

Chapter One

Wide Awake

The sun shone in through the window beside his bed as Zach pulled the sheet over his eyes. He sat up quickly as he prepared to scream and he realized where he was. He looked around his bedroom and the reality sat in; he was home again.

As he looked over at the bedside table, he saw his alarm clock, which was about to go off. He reached over and hit the button on top as he flopped over in his bed. "It was all a dream; I am home like always."

As Zach finished his last words, the Sandman watched from the corner of the bedroom. A sinister smile crossed his face. "Don't feel so safe. I am not done with you yet."

The Sandman studied his prey, realizing he should have used more sand. If he had, Zach would have remained in Dream Land. This was a mistake he would not make again. When night returned, he would be ready. The Sandman ran his hand through his side pouch and let the fine sands fall between his fingers. He wanted to grab hold of the boy and drag him back. In the light of day, that was not possible, his power was limited. He would have to wait.

Zach turned to sit on the edge of his bed, as the sheet fell in folds around him. He was trying to convince himself it was all a dream. How could it be anything else. He stretched, and the muscles of his young body flexed. He felt more toned than before. As he ran his hand down his left arm, he could see the muscle tone. This was new to him, being he was not very athletic.

As he stood up and looked in the full-length mirror that hung just behind his door, he saw his legs look more defined. As he stood there in his underwear, he stared in disbelief at the change in himself. As he grabbed his clothes and prepared to dress, he noticed more changed to his body. Looking up, he stared at his own face. He was growing a slight beard. He laughed, because he was never able to do this before. He was beginning to believe there was more going on, than he was willing to admit.

As Zach rounded the corner heading to the kitchen, he realized his mother was nowhere to be found. She was always there waiting for him, to be off to college in the morning. He shook it off as strange and grabbed some cereal for breakfast. He was starving, as if he had not eaten in days.

As he reached for his food and grabbed his drink, he felt odd. It was as if he had never used his body before. He felt clumsy and unbalanced. At times, he would slow his movements, so he did not knock things over. "What the hell is going on?" he whispered as he cleaned up his mess and headed to the college. He had to be there on time for his new cross-country running class. He been late too many times before, if it happened again the coach would kill him,

As Zach locked his car, he sprinted towards the building. His movements were more intense as he launched himself. As his shoes dug into the ground, he could feel himself fly forward. The new muscles in his legs flexed like he had never felt before. Zach was at the door before he realized, just slowing down before he crashed into it.

As he entered the gym, he looked back at the distance he traveled so quickly. Shaking his head, he was beginning to accept, he had changed. Perhaps the dream was not a dream after all. He wondered if he did go to this place, and if so, what happened to him there? How long was he trapped?

Zach joined his group as he prepared to warm up with the others. The coach led them to the indoor track, and lined them up. As the whistle cut through the air, Zach took off. He was never the fastest when compared to his fellow runners. Today was different. As he flew forward, his muscles flexed as if he had been training for a race his whole life. He flew past the other runners one by one leaving them in his wake. As the students who had been the fastest look up, they saw Zack pull to the front and finish the run.

At the finish, he looked back to see the others still coming his way. The coach joined him, as he looked Zach up and down. "How.....How did you do that?" he asked. "Ummm, I guess I am getting better." Zach answered.

The team stared at Zach in disbelief as he continued with class. His ability to run had increased so much more than he thought he was capable of. He had a hard time believing it himself. As class ended, he felt almost relieved to be leaving, after all the disgruntled looks he received, it was time to go home.

As he released the lock on the car, he looked down at his body. He almost did not recognize himself. Something had changed him, or maybe he thought, he was still dreaming. Was he still stuck in Dream Land? If the place was as dangerous as Daniel said, could it affect him mentally? Maybe coming home was all a dream.

Mullins

Chapter Two

In Dream Land

Zach screeched into the driveway of his home just like he had done a million times, but today did not feel right. He didn't even feel right in his own skin. In his brain he ran over and over the time he believed he was in the Dream Land. He only remembered a few hours, but his body had aged. He ran his fingers over the muscles he had acquired. "A person would need months of training, to reshape a body like this." As he leaned forward, he pounded his head on the steering wheel.

On the last bounce, he jarred the surface so hard that the horn sounded. Throwing himself backwards, he scanned the house expecting his mother to come running to see if he was OK. But as he watched...nothing. "This is wrong." he whispered.

Zach cautiously climbed from the car seat and headed across the lawn. Along the way he suspiciously looked around the house and through the windows. His mother was gone, but this was not normal.

As he approached her bedroom window, he looked in to find her lying on the bed. Above her stood a man holding a handful of glowing gold dust which he gently let fall upon her head. As each grain fell, it disappeared into her skin. The man was dressed in an old army fatigue style jump suit, with glowing goggles over his eyes. He looked like something from World War 2. Zach watched his mother as she lay there in a dream state, as unescapable as the Dream Land Zach had been in. If not for Daniel, he would still be there.

Zach stared intently, not knowing what to do or any way to help her. He wondered how long she had been this way. Over and over again, he reminded himself she was not being hurt; she was just sleeping. She could be awakened.

As Zach struggled to hide himself, he saw the glow entering the room. Just to the side of the bed the yellowish glow grew and shaped until there was what he believed, was a door. He leaned into the side of the house almost losing his balance, when a young girl opened the door that had formed. She was probably 15 years of age, with brown hair pulled back in a pony tail. Joining the Sandman who stood over the bed, she stared at him in confusion.

"What are you doing?" The girl insisted.

"Just making sure she stays this way long enough for us to reclaim the boy." He said as a crooked smile crossed his lips.

"You're using too much sand. You will hurt her." The girl grabbed his hand.

"Get off me bitch." I know what I am doing."

"Adam, we are not here to hurt anyone. That is not our job. We are only meant to inspire dreams."

"You know Lacey, you have always been so naïve. Things are changing. The days of the old Sandman are gone. Soon we will not have to be trapped in the Dream Land. These ones have untapped power. The more dreams we steal, the stronger will get. Then we will conquer this realm."

"No! You can't do this. We are not gods. I will stop you."

Adam laughed at her, as he dumped the remaining sand from his hand. "There are more of us, than there are of you."

Zach looked on in disbelief, as his mother's body tossed back and forth. He knew he had to do something, but what? Lacey ran back through the portal door, as Adam spun around and tore out after her. Zach flew from his hiding spot, not seeing the blue light from within his mother's bedroom.

Chapter Three

Enter the Sandman

As Zach ran down the hall, he heard the sounds from within. His mother was calling out in her induced dream state. As he flew through the doorway, he tried to stop, but his feet continued to slide forward to the end of the bed. He looked up to see Daniel standing before him. As he tried to speak, his words were buried under his heavy breathing.

"Daniel, please help." Zach belted out as he fell to his knees.

"What did they do to her?" Daniel spoke as he touched her forehead.

"The Sandman was here, well, two of them. Except one was a girl. She tried to stop the first man who was dropping golden sand onto my mother's head. When the girl challenged him, he dumped a handful onto her. Then she started thrashing back and forth. Do you know how to save her?"

"I don't know if I can reverse what he did. I am not a Sandman and I do not have the ability to reverse his actions. From what I know, she can wake up from this, but only when the effects of the sand wear off. Since there was a huge amount, it could take hours or days." Daniel said as he sat down on the corner of the bed and tried to console Zach.

"If you cannot fix this, can a Sandman?"

"Perhaps if we had one. But how do we get one to come here?'' Daniel asked.

"They left through the portal at the side of the bed. Can we do something to reopen it and go through ourselves. If we can capture one of them, maybe we can force them to come back here." Zach was determined to find a way.

"Show me where the portal was." Daniel looked on as Zach walked to the spot.

"Here." Zach answered as he dragged his foot across the floor.

Daniel walked to the spot and studied it closely. "There is still sand here. We just have to charge it and we can follow their path into the Dream World."

"This is too crazy. I woke up in my bed this morning, like everything was normal. It's just, I knew it wasn't. Things were different, hell, I am different, my own body has changed." Zach raged on not taking a breath. "How long was I in that place. How did I get back here? Explain to me what is going on! …And don't start your cryptic answer crap, I want the truth."

"Sit down and breathe. You are going to need it. You were away for a long time. Time in the other universe travels differently. A few hours here are like months there. You probably don't remember much because when you crossed back over, the trauma probably wiped a bit of your memory. It will come back, but it is probably better if you did not remember what happened to you. I have been protecting you since you arrived there. The funny thing is, as you age in the Dream Land, your body here changes and grows."

"Is that why I have all these muscles?" Zach said as he looked down.

"Yes, you have the benefit of fighting for your life. For months, you fought to survive, and in the process, your body changed. Sadly, you also aged. Your soul is older than your body. It stayed in a dream state and did not experience your life. Now it has to catch up with you. Look at it this way, it could have been worse. You could have been there for a decade or more."

Daniel chose his words carefully. He knew Zach was not ready for the whole story, or why they had come to know each other in the first place. His secret would have to wait, and in time he would reveal it.

Daniel gathered as much of the dust together as he could. From what was on the bed and floor, there was nearly a cup.

"Is it enough? Zach asked.

"It will have to be. I can't find anymore." Daniel hid his concern.

"Why were you in the other place?"

"I had business in the Dream Land. There was someone there I was trying to find and bring home. I had been there for a long time. Still couldn't find her." Daniel Answered.

"Does she mean something to you?" Zach tried not to be too pushy, but he still wanted to know.

"Yeah, she means everything to me. She was taken by a Sandman. That is how I learned how to do things like this. I have been on their trail for more time than I would like to admit. But if I didn't do that, we would not have the advantage of doing this."

Daniel allowed a faint smile to cross his face, and the sand fell from his hand. As the particles hit the floor, they collected and formed a line. The they took shape turning into the frame and then a door solidified. The portal was ready, the amount a sand was just enough.

Zach turned back to his mother. "Will she be alright until we return?"

"I believe so. She just has to survive the nightmare the Sandman planted in her head. It's not real you know. It is like a hypnotic suggestion. It can only hurt you if you believe it is real."

Zach walked to his mother's side and leaned down to kiss her, as a tear fell from his cheek. "Mom, if you can hear me, it's not real. You will beat this, and I will be back home with you soon. I love you."

As Zach walked back to the door, Daniel touched it and it began to open. Inside, a golden light swirled and twisted. "You ready for this?" Daniel asked. "Do I have a choice?" Zach replied. Daniel smiled at him as he laid a hand on Zach's shoulder, and told him to hold on. Together their forms entered the light and the door closed behind them. They were gone and the sand from the doorframe slowly disappeared.

Chapter Four

If You Die in The Void

A burst of light blinded Zach as he fell hard onto the stone surface. He opened his eyes wide, trying to focus on his surroundings. His attempt was in vain, all he could see was stars and lights swirling. He wondered if his condition was because he entered the Dream Land with his body intact. It didn't really matter; he was there and he had to gather himself together.

"Daniel, are you here?" He called out, but there was no reply. He quickly ran his hands over the surface of where he landed. Maybe there was a sign to his position.

As he ran his fingers over the cold stone surface, he could feel ridges and shapes. He knew the feel of this place. He wondered if he was surrounded by statues in a park or maybe worse, a cemetery. He ran his hand up the side of an object that felt like flowing robes. Yes, this was a statue, maybe an angel of sorts.

As he looked up where his hand had passed, the light swirl in his eyes changed and he began to see shadows. All around him there were figures. He thought it was strange that there were so many statues in one place. He thought, even stranger was that one of the statues seemed to be moving.

Zach scooted backward as he strained to focus his eyes. It was moving, and it was large. All he could make out were the black flowing robes that surrounded the dark black figure.

As Zach's eyes took focus, he saw the figure before him. It was a wraith, he knew it. He had seen them before in movies and even read of their existence in books. He shook his head, and thought it could not be real. He scrambled to his feet, still wobbly from his journey there, and backed slowly away from the creature.

As he moved backwards, an angel's arms reached down to him. Zach let out a scream as he was sure the angel's hands had embraced him. "No!" he screamed. As he turned to look behind him, the angel tipped her head forward and her facial expression changed as if she was smiling at him.

"What the hell is going on here?" He yelled at the top of his lungs. "This can't be real."

"But of course, it can. In Dream Land, anything is possible." The words sounded from the cold stone statue. It was a real as he was, just not as alive.

"What do you want from me?" He breathed deeply trying to form words.

"Nothing much, just your life force. It's what keeps us alive. Don't worry, you will simply become one of us. You will join the force that maintains the void. It won't hurt…. much." The angel's expression changed and turned psychotic as she looked up to the wraith.

Zach gathered his wits. He had no intention of staying in this screwed up dream world. He backed away from the statue and ran to the closed path, away from where he was. As he sprinted at full speed, the wraith locked onto his path, and lifted from the ground flying after him. From behind, he heard the angel's words mocking him, "You won't get away, the wraith never walks away without his quarry."

Zach ran until the stone path began to disappear. He reached the edge of a grassy landscape as he tripped over something in the dirt. He looked down at the silver shiny object. As he reached for it, he dislodged the dirt to reveal a metal helmet. He studied the object as he saw other pieces. They all would assemble as a suit of armor. "Why would there be a knight here? This makes no sense, but nothing here makes sense."

He looked up as the wraith descended from the sky above him. It spoke no words; it did not have to. The creature was all powerful. Zach was strong for a human, but in Dream Land, that meant little.

The wraith stretched out his arms and flung his robes to the side as a powerful dark light emerged from within. Zach tried to scream, but the words were absorbed into the black field that was being created to surround his body. As the creature looked downward, Zach could feel the life within him being drug out, like he was being absorbed by a black hole. He could not pull away. His body was being torn at an atomic level. He felt his bones begin to vibrate as blackness covered his eyes. He was sure he was dying.

Mullins

Chapter Five

A Light in the Darkness

As the Wraith wrapped Zach in its dark cocoon, the last moments of his life were fading away. The creature leaned in, savoring its conquest, not paying attention to its surroundings. The blue light came from behind as Daniel emerged.

"Get away from him you bitch!" Daniel screamed.

A screeching shrill voice emerged deep from withing the wraith, "No, he is mine. I have claimed him. You have no power here." Then the wraith went back to its task.

Daniel raised a hand and aimed for the black mass, and deep from within, he emitted a blast of white light. The power of the light was greater than that of the darkness. The creature loosened its grip as Daniel drew more power.

From within, the creature let go of Zach and his body fell to the ground. Daniel ran to him as the wraith withdrew. He had won, but he was fearful he had not reached Zach in time. Daniel fell to his feet and grabbed hold of him, searching for any sign of life. Deep within he found it, a faint heartbeat. Somehow Zach was alive.

"Zach, I know you are in there. If you can hear me, you have to fight and regain consciousness. We have to find a safe place for you to heal. If you can hear me, give me a sign please." Daniel held tight to Zach's hand as he waited.

"I'm still here, but just barely." Zach tried to laugh but his body was shaken to its core.

"Just a few yards from here, is a temple. It is safe and nothing can enter. We would be safe while you rest. I just need to get you there. I am going to need to get you to your feet. Can you help with that?" Daniel asked.

"I can't walk. But maybe if you let me lean on you, we can get there." Zach knew he was being hopeful. He had never felt this weak in his life. He hoped the power within the Dream Land would speed his healing somehow.

"Ok, I will help you up, and on three we try to walk. One, two…three." Daniel spoke as he searched the land around them to see if the wraith had returned, or if any other unwanted guests had arrived. They were safe, but not for long. Dream Land would send other creatures for Zach.

As they crossed the grassy landscape, Daniel drug Zack. It was more this way, than the idea that they would walk together. Daniel struggled, but he made sure they made it into the doorway safely. Inside, he passed his hand over where stones were laid together on a shelf. Instantly a shield covered the door and any other entrances to the temple.

As Daniel kneeled beside him, Zach opened his eyes. "You saved me."

"I don't know about saved. Let's just say I got there in time to stop you from dying." Daniel laughed.

"In any case, thank you…again. You seem to always be there when I need you." Zach spoke as he reached out to shake Daniel's hand.

"I haven't saved you yet. I just found a place of safety. When I get you home and all this is over, then you can thank me."

"What is this place? How did you know to come here?" Zach asked.

"This is a protected zone in the Dream Land. There are a few of them around. We were lucky that we were near this place."

"How is it you know so much about Dream Land?"

"I have been here a long time looking for Jen. She has been lost here for over a year. Every time I think I am closing in on her, the void changes things and I can't find her in time." Daniel hung his head, trying not to show his pain.

"Maybe we will find Jen and free my mom at the same time. We can work together?" Zach tried to force a smile across his darkened face. His lips quivered for a second as he breathed deeply.

"Right now, you need to rest. The forcefield will protect us through the night."

As Zach laid down on the cool floor, he felt his body changing. He thought Daniel was right, he would be better in the morning. He had no other choice. A second battle with the dark would be the end for him. His spirit was on the line the first time he entered the Dream Land, this time it was so much more.

Mullins

Chapter Six

Like Sands Through An Hour Glass

Zach fell hard into sleep, while Daniel watched over him. It was not long until Zach began to twitch. He body thrashed back and forth and he traveled deeper into dream state.

As Daniel watched, he could see subtle healing occurring, but he knew by morning it would not be enough. He had to do something to speed it all along. As Daniel studied Zach, he knew he had to take action. "I guess as long as you cannot see me do this, I am still within the rules to heal you."

Daniel held a hand above Zach and emitted a golden glow over his body. Immediately the protective coating started to make changed to Zach's body. His skin changed back to its normal color, while the energy seeped deep into his body to heal him from the inside out."

Daniel was sure he had done the right thing. Zach would survive, but there was more that had to be done. He was torn if he should play with something from the realm, but he had to show Zach the truth. There was only one way to do it. On the floor of the temple, hidden in the shadows of a corner was a leather pouch. A Sandman's pouch, and it look full.

Daniel reached for the pouch, as he looked at Zach in his fitful sleep. He hated to inflict the sand on his new friend, but there was no other way to show him a past that has been covered up.

Reaching inside the faded leather bag, he took a hand full of the sand and moved towards Zach's head. "Forgive me." He whispered, as he allowed the sand to fall over his friend. The light golden particles reflected the energy they contained as the dust was absorbed by Zach's skin. "Remember what has been hidden from you."

Daniel waited as Zach's dreams were hijacked, returning him to his childhood. He opened his eyes, in what would have been a dream to see a Sandman in his room. Zach watched a five-year-old version of himself being manipulated by the sand.

His dream jumped forward years, the same routine was happening again. None of this was new to him. Each time, the Sandman who visited erased his memory of the events. Zach watched as the dreams moved forward. Year after year, he had been violated and his memories wiped. It was all making sense to him now. He had been used for a purpose. He was destined to end up in Dream Land.

Then he came to the last night. Zach watched as he moved through the dream, then something happened he did not know. His mother interrupted the Sandman. That is why he remembered it. His mother stopped it all. And the Sandman went after her instead. He now knew so much, that had been hidden from him. He had lived two lives for so many years.

Zach shook his head, wondering how many other people they had done this to. His anger grew as he breathed deeper and deeper. He had to wake up and regain his strength. He would make them pay for what they did.

Zach watched the last moments of his travel to the Dream Land. He saw the power of the Sandman and the others of his kind. If they had used the Dream Land to obtain their powers, then why couldn't he. He just had to find a way to harness the power and hold it. If the Sandman charged their sand to control their surroundings, then he was sure he could too.

Zach jerked violently as he fought his way back to his body, and with a blink of his eyes, he awakened. He turned to look Daniel in the face. "You sent me back to my dreams, didn't you?" he asked.

"I had to do it. I didn't see any other way. I had to make you see what they did. If I had told you, then you might not have believed me. I figured if you saw it for yourself, maybe you would." Daniel spoke sadly.

"I understand. You did what you had to. Did you use that to send me back?"

Daniel shook his head yes. "Can you deal with this?"

"Yes, I can deal with it. And with this bag, I can even the playing field." Zach said angrily.

Mullins

Chapter Seven

The Lost One

Deep within a darkened passageway, a teenage girl shook her head, trying to break the darkness that had her under its spell for months. She shook back and forth trying to fight her way out of the groggy state that had become her norm. She did not belong there in the depths of darkness. A Sandman brought her to Dream Land and intended to keep her there,

As she pressed her back against the wall behind her, she tried to push up and get to her feet. Her efforts were in vain, being she had been loaded with sand. The Sandman was thorough and poured enough sand to keep a normal girl comatose for months, but what he did not understand, Jen was no normal girl.

She felt trapped, only her mind responded to her movements. Her body was in a state she could only fight for simple actions. She sat back up and, in her mind, began to meditate. She had always been good at it. If she was to get free, she would have to be at peace mentally.

In her mind she thought of the one who had always been her savior. She and Daniel had been together so long. She loved him more than anyone she had ever known. From the life she had led, he was what she was most proud of. She had walked through life and death with him and still they came out together.

As she remembered him and the fight where he was almost killed, she remembered the power of healing. She used it to help others, but never to help herself. She didn't know if it was possible.

As she sat on the floor, she managed to pull her legs into a crossed position and lowered her hands on top of them. Jen chose her focal point. She remembered the light, and the abilities it had given her as she began to tap into her inner power.

As the darkness of the hall encompassed her, she tapped into the light. She struggled to maintain control as her eyes flew open and the brightness of the light shined out, lighting the area in front of her. As she chanted, the light swirled around her, and she began to glow a dim light. She had achieved control, and she was determined to not let go.

In a matter of minutes, the entire hall glowed from the light her body was emitting. As the power grew, her chanting got louder. Her power flashed out like a small star, lighting the way. Holding her focus, her body levitated into the air, and began to spin in a circle.

Jen had achieved her goal; she was healing and the Sand was being forced out of her body. As she lowered her legs, the spinning stopped and she found herself landing on her feet. Her eyes slowly returned to normal, showing the normal colors of her hazel eyes.

Jen smiled as she realized what she had done. "Hah, I did it. I knew I had it in me somewhere. And they say Daniel is the strong one. Now, I just have to get out of here and find him. But where am I?" Jen looked around; this place was unfamiliar.

She looked in each direction. She could move now, but being she was asleep when she arrived, this was all foreign. As she stood there, she felt a cool breeze cross her cheek. If there was a breeze, it had to have come from an opening. She was sure of that.

Turning to her left, she began her journey towards what she hoped was an opening. She walked for what she imagined to be forever. There were no markings on the wall. No signs of anyone being there for years.

After hours of walking, she saw a light. It was small and far in the distance but she knew it had to be the opening. She was never so happy to see daylight. A slight smile crossed her face as she anticipated freedom. Her body had healed. She felt at home in her own mind again.

The endless walking was beginning to be too much for her to take. As she looked behind her and then all around, she knew there was a shortcut. "What the hell, who will know?" She spoke under her breath. Jen envisioned the opening she saw, and herself being there. Clenching her fists, she drew upon the power she hid inside. She was told never to use her abilities in front of humans, but here, she was sure she was alone.

A shaft of light formed around her and she disappeared within it. At the end of the tunnel her light re-formed as she stepped out into the light of the outside. She hadn't used her abilities much and without a focal point, she would have still been walking the tunnel. Her gamble paid off.

"I did it," She giggled to herself as she walked out and looked at the landscape.

"Yes, you did it little one. Your power led me straight to you." The Wraith said drawing down upon her.

"What the hell are you?" Jen asked.

"Your worst nightmare, I would imagine."
He responded.

"Nice try, I have faced my worst nightmare.
He was a demon from Hell itself and I kicked his ass.
So, you will have to try a little harder to intimidate
me." Jen was confident in her lack of fear.

"We'll see about that." The Wraith
challenged her.

Jen spun around and looked for escape
options and prepared to defend herself. As the
Wraith spread his arms and his power began to form
from within his robes, Jen clenched her fists. This
was one battle she was ready for. After all the time
she had been forced to sleep in the hidden hallway,
she had power in reserve.

She stepped back, and as the Wraith blasted
her and tried to rob her of her life force. Jen let loose
a blast of energy aimed at the Wraith. As her power
hit, the Wraith knew he had underestimated his
adversary.

Jen stepped forward one step at a time, as she closed in on the dark figure. "You thought I was weak because I was a girl, didn't you? I promise, this is one mistake you will regret." Jen let go of all her anger as she struck a crippling blow to the Wraith. As it fell to the ground, she turned and walked away.

"Never underestimate someone because they are smaller than you." Jen grumbled under her breath. She then stepped into a beam of light, which carried her far off into the distance, and away from the black heap she had left on the ground.

Mullins

Chapter Eight

The Journey to The Queen

Zach and Daniel set off early from their safe place. The temple could shield them, but they had to find their way to the Sandman layer. Zach's mother had to be freed, and Daniel would not give up until he was reunited with Jen.

As they walked, they passed so may distorted placed that looked as if they were born of nightmares. Some places were filled with death and the dead bodies it left behind. Daniel looked on as they passed a graveyard, and he thought back to his own past. The memories were still fresh, even though he had tried to bury them deep in a place where he could deal with them. He had a new life now, and that was with Jen. If he could ever find her.

As they climbed over the next hill, the saw a bright flash of light. Daniel knew it all too well.

There was someone there who had the ability to orb. His heart leapt as he hoped it was Jen. They saw the battle from a distance. It was too far from where they were to know for sure what was going on.

"We have to go that way!" Daniel ordered him.

"What could that be? Maybe it is something dangerous. I'm not sure about this." Zach tried to change Daniel's mind.

"No, I know what I am talking about. We have to go there." Daniel was sure of it.

They traveled for hours before they reached the site of the battle. There on the ground, lay the remains of a Wraith. Daniel leaned over and studied it, making sure it was dead. There was nothing left there to fear. Whoever had killed it did a good job.

"What could kill a Wraith?" Zach said looking nervously at Daniel.

"Someone of great power. A power of good. We have nothing to fear from this person." Daniel tried to hide what he really knew. This was Jen's handywork. She was alive, and he was sure now that he could find her. His doubts were erased.

"What do we do now?" Zach asked.

"We find the Wraith killer. There is safety in numbers you know." Daniel answered.

Daniel looked over the area until he found what he was looking for, a faint trace of orb. He had a direction in which Jen had gone. They sat out in the direction he pointed out. Zach did not understand how Daniel could know how to track this person, but he had never steered Zach wrong before.

The trail was strong for a long time and them faded near the gates of a huge settlement. From the outside it was surrounded with great walls and embattlements. Daniel studied it hard, he knew places like this. This was the home of a guild. They would not be welcome there. He pulled at Zach's shoulder.

"We need to get out of here before we are seen. It may not be safe." Daniel insisted.

"It looks fine. They aren't attacking us or anything."

"No, not yet. Sometimes it is better to be safe than sorry. Let's go."

As they walked past, they kept hidden in the tree line near the edge of the small city. Inside they heard voices and the sounds of soldiers as if they were rallying to meet someone. They did not know what, and they did not want to know.

Inside the wall, Jen stood, while the soldiers assembled around her. They did not come aggressively; she was welcomed to their settlement. She became their honored guest. Outside the walls, Daniel moved on, and found a direction for them to follow. Deep inside him, he felt a spark. It was a familiar one, but weaker than he had ever known. Dreamland was dampening his ability to use his power of location. He was sure he was near Jen. He just had no way to call out to her.

As they followed the path down towards the river nearby, they heard the beats of hooves against the ground. There were horses coming. Daniel grabbed tight to Zach's arm and dragged him down off the side of the embankment. Down under a tree's roots, they found a hiding place. It was there they awaited their capture. Daniel drew deep into the roots as he heard the hooves stop just above them. Neither of them dared to breathe as they listened to the voices of the riders.   They had been seen.

Mullins

Chapter Nine

On the Run

"They have to be here somewhere. I know I saw them heading this way." The one soldier said scanning the area around them.

"Perhaps, but I see nothing now." The other responded. "Maybe we should search down by the water."

Daniel's heart beat faster. He knew if the soldiers came down further, their hiding place would be in plain sight. His mind raced for a safe way out, but there was nothing he could do that would not reveal himself or his abilities.

Above on the ground, the sound of hooves moving back echoed down on top of them. Daniel looked at Zach, who was clinching the bag of sand. He could not be allowed to witness what had to be done. There was no way to avoid, it was one person seeing him or two others. He knew the rules, and humans witnessing the use of power was forbidden.

"Zach, they are going to find us. Which leaves me in a position I don't want to be in. Can you agree to do exactly as I say?" Daniel asked.

"Yeah, what do you want me to do?" Zach asked with a confused look on his face.

"Just close your eyes, and do not open them until I tell you to."

Zach closed his eyes, even though he wanted to watch what was about to happen. He trusted Daniel and he did as he was asked. Daniel reached out and put his hand on Zach's arm. Around them formed a blue light that engulfed them.

Daniel searched his mind for some place within Dream Land where they could orb. His mind went to so many places he had visited. He feared the landscape might have changed, being so much in the void changed daily. The he locked onto a place he had been before, full of city buildings. They had been assembled like a small city, each one floating in the clouds.

Daniel closed his eyes and envisioned the buildings. He initiated their orb, and the light around them flashed brilliantly. As the soldiers came down the side of the embankment, they saw the blinding light. For a second both their visions were clouded, and then when they returned to normal, they saw nothing. With nothing to see, they continued looking.

The blue orb containing Daniel and Zach, flashed to the floating city. The light formed just on the edge of a sidewalk that was in pieces. The city looked like pieces of a puzzle put together by someone who had no idea what the whole picture should have looked like,

Some buildings floated higher than others, while sidewalk pieces floated in open air. Nothing quite matched up. Some of the buildings were damaged, possibly from war. They could have come from different time periods. There did not seem to be people living there, but how could they? Nothing was very stable.

Daniel looked on, as he sat the orb down on what he thought was a solid form. As the shield disappeared. He let go of Zach's hand and told him it was OK to open his eyes. As Zach moved to get his footing, the sidewalk beneath him started to crumble. With nothing to grasp, he began to fall. He let out a scream as Daniel turned to help him.

Zach called for help, as he started to move. To his surprise, he fell upwards. Just as the buildings did, he floated in the space of the city. He was so confused; this place was like a crazy nightmare he wanted to escape.

Daniel jumped up and grabbed his hand, before he floated too far away. "I've got you, just hold on."

As Daniel pulled him down, his feet returned to the sidewalk as if gravity had returned to his body and surroundings. Zach put his hands to his head and screamed. He turned to Daniel and laughed. He had no words to describe how he felt.

"You thought this was better than getting caught by the soldiers?" Zach asked sarcastically.

"We didn't get captured.   I say that is better." Daniel snapped back.

"And how do we get off this weird sidewalk floating in the cloud city?" Zach demanded an answer.

"Look, it was the first place I thought of that would be abandoned. So technically, it is a ghost town in the sky, not a cloud city."

They both began to laugh, as the sidewalk started to move. Both dropped to their knees and held on, as the block of cement gained speed. Watching as the sidewalk took aim at a building, they flew faster than before. It was going to slam into the side wall directly in front of them.

Daniel turned to Zach, "When I tell you, jump. Maybe we can make it to that balcony."

Zach shook his head and as the cement slab slammed into the building, they both jumped. Daniel landed in the cement opening that covered the edge. Zach was not so lucky, his hand missed as he reached out. His body spun away from the building, and there was no way for him to stop his ascent.

Chapter Ten

You Can Never Leave

Jen explored the small city enclosed by the wall. She studied the architecture of the place, and decided it was medieval feeling. She laughed to herself, "They could have filmed Lord of The Rings here."

As Jen turned towards the front gate, she saw the riders returning from their scouting run. She made her way towards them, hoping of news of Daniel. She felt him nearby, after she entered the wall, they he just seemed to disappear. She couldn't feel him at all after that.

Jen approached the riders, hopeful of good news. "Hello, I do not mean to bother you, but while you were on patrol, did you see a blond boy just outside the wall?" She asked them.

"Yes, and no. I thought I saw someone for a minute. Then they disappeared. All I can say is, we saw a bright blue light, that blinded us for a time. Then it was gone as fast as it started."

"Thank-you very much." Jen said smiling at the soldiers as she turned away. It was Daniel, she was sure of that. Who else could emit that kind of light? He must have orbed, she thought to herself. She was sure of that. He was looking for her.

As Jen walked on, she saw an old woman making her way in the same direction. As Jen slowed the old woman came closer. She reached out her hand, which held baked cookies. She smiled at Jen as if to offer her one.

"Do you want me to have this?" Jen asked softly.

"Yes, my dear, they are especially for you. Please eat." The old woman insisted.

"Thank-you. I appreciate you offering them to me." Jen tried to be friendly, but as she took hold of the cookie, she had a vision flash through her head. She had always been empathic, but recently her abilities had increased exponentially.

In her vision, she saw the old woman using magic to control and enslave others. The cookie was infused with a poison. Jen thought to herself, "What kind of screwed up fairytale land have I ended up in?"

As the old woman watched intently Jen held the cookie in her hand and pretended to eat. She turned away as if to admire the buildings, and slipped pieces of the cookie into her pocket. Before long, she had made the whole cookie disappear.

"Thanks so much for making me feel welcome, but I think it is time I continued on my journey." Jen said as she turned away and began to walk.

The old woman ran up behind her. "No dear one, you are not leaving." She said in a cracked demented voice.

"What are you talking about. I can leave anytime I want." Jen insisted.

"No, you are mine now. When you ate the cookie, you surrendered to me. You cannot leave." The old woman screamed at her.

"Nice game you are playing there. But you just tried it on the wrong girl. I am not a mere human, and as far as your cookie was concerned, here…you can have it back." Jen reached into her pocket and presented the broken pieces of the cursed cookie. "Oh, and by the way, you can drop the disguise. I can see through your illusion. Old lady, my butt."

With a wave of Jen's hand, the disguise faded and the true woman emerged. She was no old lady at all, but a young witch who had used the ruse for years to take victims. Jen stood back and looked her up and down.

"I will not be your next victim. Now back off, I am leaving." Jen insisted.

"How did you do this, no one has ever seen through my masquerade."

"Let's just say, you aren't the only one with a few tricks up her sleeve. Now, as I said, I am leaving." Jen backed up a few feet and smiled at the witch. Then by clenching her fists and imagining the land outside the wall, she raised her shield and an orb formed. A bright light filled the area and then she was gone.

The witch walked over and observed the ground where Jen had stood. There was nothing to show she was ever there. The witch's magic was strong, but Jen had more power. Outside the wall Jen continued her journey searching for Daniel's orb trail.

Mullins

Chapter Eleven

Escape the Cloud City

Daniel watched as Zach got further away. He looked around for something, anything that could be used to ride the cloud current. He saw on the floor of the terrace beside him, was a broken piece of wood. He thought it might have once been a surfboard. Daniel snatched it up and held it just beside the building. It floated; he could barely contain himself.

Reaching out, he pulled the board to himself and climbed onboard. Still holding onto the side of the building, he aimed the board in Zach's direction. "I am not asking for a miracle, but let this work." On his last word, Daniel launched the board.

He drifted slowly at first, then in a moment of desperation, he held a hand behind himself and shot out a blast of energy. The board moved quickly through the air. As he ascended, Zach turned to see him trailing behind. Zach yelled out, as the board came near enough to jump onto.

"Are you always going to be here to save me?" Zach asked him.

"We are on a mission together; I can't let you down. Besides, it was kind of my fault. I didn't get you close enough to get onto the balcony."

"Yeah, we need to talk about that. Exactly how did you get us from the river to the cloud city?"

"In time my friend, I will explain it all. But for now, pay attention. I think that building, is our new landing spot." Daniel called out as the board carried them into an opening in the west side of the building that looked like it had been bombed once in a war.

The board hit the side of the structure and flipped inside throwing the boys onto the remaining floor of that level. Daniel rolled hard towards the side of the building, catching himself before he fell out of the opening. Zach landed near him, grabbing quickly to Daniel's hand.

The two sat breathing heavily, as they watched several bricks from the building float away. They turned to each other knowing how lucky they were. Daniel's heart settled as he tried to stand up. They were both unnerved by the way the building bobbed back and forth in the air currents. The both agreed the feeling was similar to being on a boat that was bouncing in a heavy wave.

"We have to get to the roof of this building." Daniel insisted. "We can see everything around us from there."

"I agree. We need to get off this level before it's is gone." Zach said as the building rocked and knocked him sideways.

"There should be stairs somewhere around here." Daniel said, as he pulled Zach behind him.

They moved into the center of the building, both scanning signs and doorways until they found what they needed. They flung open the door and studied the stairs. The steps going to the upper level seemed to be intact. Slowly they climbed being careful of the disintegrating building.

The two did well, only having to avoid piles of debris. When they reached the 12th floor everything changed. A large corner of the building was ripped away. From the dark black scoring, it was during a war.

"What do we do now? The side of the building with the stairs is gone?" Zach asked.

"We have to find a way up. If the wall is solid enough, we could climb it to the next level." Daniel suggested.

"Yeah, or you could just grab ahold of a floating piece of brick and ride it to god knows where." The female voice came from above.

Daniel's lit up. He didn't need to see her face. Jen had found him. From above in the opening, a fire hose started to descend through a hole in the floor. Daniel reached for the hose first and got ready to climb.

After he was to the top, he told Zach to come up. As the both reached safety, Daniel turned to their savior. Jen emerged from the shadows and walked towards him.

"Is it really you?" He asked.

"You know it, bright eyes. I couldn't sit around and wait for you to save me. I escaped and trailed you here. Who's your friend?"

"Jen this is Zach, he is here to free his mother from a Sandman."

"Hi, it's a long story. I will tell you as we climb to the roof." Zach went on to explain.

They climbed the last few levels, until they found the roof. The three of them moved to a side wall, and looked out over the insane landscape of buildings floating near and below them. The buildings floated freely into the sky, almost waiting to crash into each other.

"So, guys where do we go from here?" Jen asked.

"I don't think that is the question. The better one is how do we get down from here?" Zach corrected her.

"We will find a way. Just like with everything since we came to this crazy place. You just have to believe there is a way," Daniel said laughing and putting his arms around Jen. "I am just glad to get you back again.

Chapter Twelve

Reunited

A shadow covered the top of the building, as three dark forms looked around in different directions. They had become uneasy, as the movements of the floating brick and mortar creation became erratic. Still, they could find no escape.

"There has to be a way down from here?" Zach called, out as he rejoined the other two in the center of the rooftop.

"I know, we will come up with something." Daniel tried to reassure him.

"You know, you never told me how you rescued me before. You said you would. What are you?" Zach pressured him for an answer.

"Zach, there are some things I am not allowed to tell you, and others I cannot do in the presence of a human. It is for your safety, and everyone else's. Just give me a minute and I will work this out."

"If we can't find a way, you always have the sand." Jen insisted.

"No, I have carried this with me for a reason. I have to save my mother, and if it takes this to convince a Sandman…so be it. We will not use it now." Zach said as he breathed deeply.

Jen turned and looked at Daniel. She was concerned for the situation at hand, but also for Zach's need for the sand. He seemed to be holding on to it, in an unhealthy way. Perhaps it was affecting him.

Jen took Daniel's hand, and walked him to the North side of the rooftop. "We have a problem here." She said looking into Daniel's eyes.

"I know, somehow the power of the sand has distorted his reason. He has been too close to it for days now. Maybe it affects humans in a different way than the Sandman."

"There are many of the Sand People right. There isn't just one Sandman." Jen asked.

"Yes, they are a group. Kind of like the Guardians or White Lighters. There initial purpose was to do good, but as you can see, it has gotten out of control. I think they are coming apart internally. There is an evil within them." Daniel explained.

"Is there no one in charge of them?"

"Not that I know of. They are a group of higher beings; who in a way, are supposed to govern dream states. They are here to inspire and nurture through dreams, kind of like a muse who keeps you healthy and on track in life. Just somewhere along the way some of them went rogue." Daniel could not keep the concerned look from his face.

"Is that how I got here?" Jen asked.

"Yeah, you were taken while still in your body, through one of the doorways. I had no idea what had happened, until you were gone. Maybe they slipped me some sand, enough to keep someone of my level in dream state."

"So, you can use the sand to make a doorway out of here?" Jen asked.

"Yes, but getting him to give it up, is the problem. I created a doorway from his home to here. That is how I brought him in with his body intact. We caught two of the Sand People dumping a huge dose of sand on his mother. They ran through the doorway they created. I scooped up enough leftover sand to create a second." Daniel retold the story as Jen became concerned.

"Why did you end up with him in the first place? It all seems too arranged. I mean, first I am taken, and then run into a human, who is traveling in and out of Dream Land. Something is not right here."

"Maybe you are right, but I do not think Zach is manipulating any of this. I was almost beginning to believe he is a charge assigned to me. Maybe I am supposed to watch over him. I just happened to be where he needed me. Your abduction is a whole other story." Daniel added.

"So, we are here in another reality, on a building floating in air, and cannot do a thing to save ourselves, because it is a violation to use our abilities in from of humans? Is that right." Jen began to get angry.

"I did do something to save him before, as he said. I just told him to close his eyes, so he could not see what was happening. Maybe I was wrong to do that." Daniel tried to make sense of it all.

"Hold on, maybe we are going about this all wrong. Maybe you could use your abilities because he isn't what he appears to be." Jen said as she grabbed tight to Daniel's arm.

"You think he is a product of this place. You mean magical?" Daniel asked.

"Oh, come on Danny, we have seen weirder things in our travels. Hell, we have even fought demons and the undead. How do we know he is not a magical creature, or at least half of one? His mother was human, maybe daddy was something else." Jen was not going to let this go. She stared across the way to Zach. She knew she had to figure him out. Something was telling her he was more than he let on.

Chapter Thirteen

We All Wear Disguises

Jen began to walk towards Zach. She was determined to learn his secret. All she had to do to read him, was touch his skin. Jen's powers of an empath were growing exponentially, and after all she had been through, she needed the truth. Not just for herself, but for Daniel as well.

"Jen, you just can't run over to him and grab hold to read him." Daniel pleaded with her.

"Wanna bet? Jen was headstrong, and she felt she had a point to make. She was sure she was right and she would prove it to Daniel.

As she came up behind Zach, he turned and looked at her confused. "Is everything OK? He asked. "Did you come up with a way to get off of here?"

"I think I might know a way. You know, I never thanked you for being here with Daniel and trying to rescue me. Would you be upset if I hugged you? Just as a thank-you." she asked.

"No, that would be alright." Zach smiled as he answered her.

Jen leaned into him and innocently put her arms around. As he hugged back, she pulled tight around his neck, as a flood of images appeared in her mind. There was a nearby garden area, where a celebration was occurring. There was to be a coronation of the new queen.

Jen held tight as the images continued to flow. She saw a middle-aged woman approaching a throne. She didn't understand why she was seeing this. The scene played out like something through the looking glass. As Jen glanced around, she was sure this was something in the near future. She just didn't know why it was attached to Zach.

As Jen held onto him, she reached back into his past. She wanted to know who Zach's father was.

Most of his memories of childhood did not include a father. She pushed deeper until he was an infant. Then a man was there.

Jen studied his features and how he would come and go, but was never a daily part of Zach's life. Then Jen hit on a memory that was buried deep within, almost a hidden pain that he chose not to bring to light.

In a room of the house where Zach grew up, his mother was arguing with the same man. He insisted he had to leave. He had business in another place, and she could not go with him. They argued as the then child Zach cried in his crib.

"Look, I have told you before. I can't take you with me. Where I am going is dangerous, you could get hurt. Besides, it is no place for a small child. Just stay here and I will return." The man nervously tried to convince her.

"You never said it would be like this. If I had known, I would have never been with you in the first place. Now, I have a child by you. It's like I have to raise him alone. You lied to me; you hid so much. Now, what the hell do I do?" She turned away as tears streamed down her face.

Jen watched as the scene played out. She had found what she came after. She just needed one final piece of the puzzle, the have her proof. The memory played on as Jen watched and waited.

"Did you ever even love me?" She asked

"Yeah, I did, I still do. But I have no control of what I have to do. I have to go back to the realm and do my duties. If I don't, they will come for you and Zach. I am not willing to let them harm either of you. I will return when I can." He tried to reassure her.

"How will I know you are coming back?" She asked.

"I don't know, but if it is in my power, I will return." He said as he touched her shoulder.

Turning to face each other, their arms wrapped around and they pulled into a passionate kiss. Neither wanted to let go, but he knew his time was running out. If he did not leave, they would track him down.

Reaching into the pocket of his trench coat, he pulled out a pair of old aviator goggles and put them over his head. Walking over to Zach, he ran his gloved fingers over the boy's head. He searched his heart for a feeling, he wanted to love the boy. He had every intention of staying in this life he created. But the Dream Land had other things in mind for him.

Reaching down to his side, he pulled back his trench coat and reached to a bag on his waist. Inside was the sand he needed to form a doorway to the other universe. As he grabbed a handful, he held his hand up in the air and moved it in the shape of a doorway as the sand began to glow and transform.

When the doorway was fully formed, he cocked his head to the side and grinned at her as he stepped through. The brightness of the doorway grew, as he was transported to the temple on the other side. He stepped out of the door and walked forward to find another Sandman waiting for him.

"Where have you been? You have been away for months." The Sandman asked.

"I had things to do." He said as he put his belongings on the stone table by the wall.

"You know they put a bounty on your head?" The Sandman asked.

"So, I guess you are here to collect it?" He knew his time was up. No one survived a bounty.

He spun around as if to jump at the Sandman, when a blast of sand blew through him. A sound came from his lips as he faced death…"Zach." Then his body was torn apart as the sand ripped through his flesh leaving nothing behind that would identify him.

When the Sandman left, all there was to say they had been there, was a bag of sand the fell in the corner of the temple.

Chapter Fourteen

Escape the Truth

As Jen pulled back from Zach, she had learned more than she expected to. She turned and looked at Daniel. She faked a smile, as she tried not to let on what she had learned. She had never liked reading another person's life. Sometimes the pain was so real, and she felt the pain just as the one she had read.

Zach had buried this memory so deeply; he probably did not know it still existed. Perhaps his mother made up a story, to explain where his father had gone and he accepted it. Jen was not sure how to approach this. How could she tell him, she knew who his father was and how he died?

When the time was right, Jen pulled Daniel to the side and explained all that she found. "Well, now you know the truth. He is part human and part

Sandman. Maybe that is why he is holding onto the bag so hard, it belonged to his father."

"You know there are days, when I miss being alive sixty or so years ago. Just being a normal teenage boy, with nothing to worry about except school dances and hanging with my friends." Daniel jabbed at her.

"Hey, are you saying you regret our life together." Jen took offense.

"Nope, you know I love you. It's just, we have been through so much, through life and death and life again. There is always some insane thing in our path. But you, I would never give up, for any of it. Who said being a higher being would be easy?" Daniel laughed out loud.

"I get your point, but what about the problems at hand?" Jen asked. "We have to get off this building, Sand Boy over there has to be told, and there is still the coronation I saw. It makes no sense, why was I shown that?"

"I guess, in time we will know." Daniel said as the roof beneath him, began to shake.

"What the hell is going on?" Zach screamed, as he scrambled to his feet.

The building vibrated, as it swayed back and forth. Something was happening to shake the cloud city. As they watched, the buildings started to sway backwards and then swing around. Their building had been steady since they arrived on the roof. Now the vibration was increasing to a state, that they could barely stand upright on its surface.

As they watched, buildings started to move towards each other. They would spin until they hit. It made no sense. Some moved more erratically than others. While a couple stood still in the air, others started to crash into each other. Daniel searched for a building that was not moving.

As he scanned the skyline, he found what he wanted. There was one building that had barely moved at all. He knew the only issue would be getting to it.

As he felt the movement of the building back and forth, he came up with a plan. If the building was already in movement, maybe he could force it to move in the direction he wanted, towards the other stationary building.

Daniel got Jen's attention, and had her distract Zach, as he grabbed hold of the edge of the rooftop. When the building swayed to the direction he wanted, Daniel held tight and released a burst of energy that sent the building drifting.

The building shook and made cracking noises as the bottom floors began to fall off. Daniel had not taken into account the instability of abuse the building had suffered. The roof seemed to be staying intact.

As the building drifted towards its destination, Daniel released another burst, to slow them down. As they came close to the other building, Daniel called for them to gather at the edge. The remains stopped within a couple of feet of hitting the new building. They were close enough to run and jump from the rooftop to a landing on the other building.

Jen flew through the air, and then Zach. As Daniel prepared to jump, the original building began to spin. He knew he would never make it. As Jen watched, she grabbed Zach's shoulder and turned him, so he could not see the blue light of Daniel orbing.

Once all three were gathered, they set out to explore the building. Climbing the stairs into the raised lobby, they did not realize they were being watched. After they climbed the stairs, small spiders came climbing from their hiding places. One by one they added to the group until hundreds trailed behind studying their prey.

Mullins

Chapter Fifteen

Into the Spiders Lair

As they entered the lobby, the spiders took to the walls and ceiling. It had been years, since they had seen such a feast. Word was sent back by a couple of scouts to alert the cluster, there would be dinner that day.

"This place is creepy." Jen insisted.

"I guess, but it is better than being crushed in the last building. I just get the feeling, we are being watched." Zach said as he looked around.

"I think that is because we are." Daniel said pointing to the walls.

The spiders covered every inch of the entry way. They ranged in size from small to large and some even mutated to huge sizes. They stared intently at their meal. Jen backed closer to Daniel, as she watched the spiders begin to close in on them.

They ran to the stairs, as the spiders scattered across the floor. Close on their heels, the spiders grew in numbers. Jen screamed; she had never seen anything like this. It was not how she planned to go out.

Reaching the next floor, they slammed the door behind them. Hoping the spiders could not get through, they searched for other ways to go through the building. The floor they were on, seemed to be sealed from their approach.

"Daniel, this was not a good place to escape death." Jen Laughed nervously.

"No, we have to find our way back to land. I am not playing with spiders." Daniel answered.

"Ok, but we have to find a way down. What can we do?" Zach asked.

"Maybe you could break out a doorway, with some of the sand in your pouch." Jen was tired of hiding the secret. It was life and death now, he had to know.

"I don't know how to do that. Daniel did it last time. Besides, I told you, I had a reason to save this."

Jen walked over to Zach. Raising a hand to his head, she spoke. "This will not hurt a bit, but I feel you have a right to know the truth about your life. As she placed her fingers upon his forehead, visions flowed from within. Zach's life was revealed.

He watched as his father walked away through the door. Then images came from his childhood, and the Sandman who visited and poured sand on his head, as he was brought to Dream Land. His memory had been blocked by the sand for years, he had made so many trips into the, as a child and then as an adult. All wiped clean, as if dreams erased from memory.

He turned to Jen, "How did you do that?" Zach stared at Jen, as if he was terrified.

"I have a gift. You needed to remember, so I gave your past back to you. It has been hidden from you for far too long, and you deserve to know what has been happening to you." Jen said as she laid a hand on his shoulder.

Zach jerked away, as he turned and looked out the huge glass window to his side. He searched his brain over and over, to justify what he had learned. He did not know how all of this was true. If all he learned was true, then he was what he had truly learned to hate, a Sandman.

"I'm sorry…. here take this. I don't want it anymore. I don't want to be a Sandman, or even half of one." Zach said as he tried to give the pouch to Jen.

"No Zach, this doesn't have to be bad. Yes, your father was something you don't approve of, but there are good Sandmen. You don't even have to be one, but you could prove them wrong, and embrace your heritage. Be a better man. Live a good life and don't let this define you." Jen tried to reassure him.

"You read me; did you see evil in me?" Zach asked.

"I saw no evil at all, just a good man who has been dealt a bad hand. So now, we help you take charge of that, and save your mother." Jen tried to calm him.

"Yeah, that is another subject, my mother, she has a lot to answer for."

"Maybe…Maybe not. I think she just wanted to protect you. She may not have known about the visits over the years." Daniel added.

As the mood shifted in the room, a banging started at the door. It started out subtly and then grew lauder and louder. The door crumbled before their eyes. The spiders filtered in growing larger and larger in size. And then the mother of all the cluster came through the door.

The huge spider stood six feet in height, a mutated monster, who was ready to entrap them all. Daniel grabbed the sand bag from Jen, and handed it to Zach. The spiders sprang forward, as Zach fumbled to open the pouch.

Running his hand inside, he grabbed a hand full of the sand and pulled it out. Holding it in the air, he moved as his newly found memories reminded him. As he completed the movement, the spiders came on top of them. Pulling the door open, the three leaped through, and landed below the cloud city on grassy land, they could have barely seen from the cloud city above.

As they scrambled to their feet, the doorway stood open. The largest of all the spiders led her cluster through to the land below. As Daniel and Zach attempted to force the doorway closed, the spiders turned to attack.

Chapter Sixteen

When Spiders Attack

As Zach leapt for the open door, the Queen Spider turned in his direction. She sprung forth and landed on top of him. Daniel watched as the spider bit into him, shooting a venomous blow that made Zach curl up on the ground. His ability to move was gone.

Daniel grabbed hold of the door as he watched the spider hover over Zach. He was successful in closing the doorway, and stopping the rest of the cluster from coming through. Jen orbed to his side as soon as she saw what was happening. They had to take out the Queen, if not Zach would become her feast.

"She is so big." Jen tried to speak.

"Yes, but together, maybe we can take her out." Daniel hoped he was right. He had never fought such a creature before. He wasn't even sure if their abilities would work on such creatures.

"I've got the right." Jen yelled as she started to run.

"I am ready when you are." Daniel yelled back.

As they took their places, they both focused their energy. As they locked on their target, a massive energy blast came from within them, and hit dead center of their goal. The power intensified as they lifted their arms, then the giant spider let out a screeching noise, just before it exploded.

Everything in the area was coated in the spider's parts, including Daniel and Jen. When the smaller spiders saw the remains of their queen, they scattered in all directions in fear of dying themselves. In minutes, all that was left were the shredded parts of the spider.

As Jen looked on in disgust, she felt an odd feeling on her back. She tried to ignore it, but soon she felt a tugging on her shirt. As she tried to turn her head to look, she felt the small hairs from a spider's leg touching her neck. She attempted to let out a scream but she was paralyzed. Daniel looked at her from a distance, unsure what was happening until the spider crawled onto Jen's shoulder. He raised a hand and took aim as he screamed, "Jen, hold still." He then blasted the spider, as Jen took a deep breath. She screamed out as the feeling returned to her body. "I hate spiders!"

"Jen, help me get him out of this." Daniel called out, as he landed on his knees beside Zach.

As Jen pulled at the silky thread like substance, it would not tear. "Daniel, this stuff is unbreakable. How can we get it off? Can he breathe in there?"

"I hope so. What if I hit it with a short blast? Not enough to hurt him, but enough to cut through." Daniel asked.

"Do we have any other choice? He could be suffocating in there." Jen replied.

Daniel stood above Zach and emitted a few small bursts of his energy. With each attempt, a layer of the webbing burned away. As the last blast flew forth, the sound of Zach choking, came forth from the cocoon.

Jen leaned over Zach and emitted a healing yellow glow which calmed him, and started to reverse the venom bites from the spider. As she worked to heal Zach, Daniel peeled away the thick coating the still clung to the boy's body.

"You're going to be OK Zach. Just hang in there a little while." Daniel tried to reassure him.

"Well, after all this, I guess hiding who we are, and can do, is not necessary." Jen laughed.

"We still have to keep a low profile. Zach may know things, but the rest of the population has no clue. Besides, I am not sure I want to flaunt that there are two White Lighters running around this crazy place. Who knows what crazy that knowledge would bring?" Daniel explained, as he stood up to scout the area. He was not sure if their fight with the spider had attracted attention.

Off in the distance, a dark figure loomed behind a stone wall. He watched intently to see where the three would go after their harrowing fight. At his feet a small spider crept, as he watched it get closer.

"Stupid little creature. You know nothing of this world." He said, as he bent over and picked it up. "You were protected by your Queen, just as I have had a Queen. Mine died, then again, so did yours. And that is where the similarity ends, for you see I have a new Queen. She will take the thrown in just a few days' time. While you will not have a new Queen. You will wonder aimlessly until something bigger than you comes along. Well, I guess that is just the order of life. Some of us live while others die. Perhaps it would be better if I just put you out of your misery."

And with his last words, he dropped the small creature. As it moved quickly, as to flee from the dark clothed Wraith, he raised a foot and slammed it down on top of the spider. "I guess today, I am the something bigger that came along. First you, then the ones you battled with. The foolish girl thought she killed me. Things don't stay dead in Dream Land for long."

Chapter Seventeen

Healing While Surrounded by Death

The Wraith made his way back to the Royal Garden. The place had been decorated and looked the part of a formal ceremony. He made his way through the passageway, allowing his long black robes to flow behind him in his wake. He traveled through the maze of flowers and shrubbery until he found…. her.

The new Queen stood with her back to him. She was adorned with the finest gown and the light reflected of her shining jewelry. The Wraith lowered his head as he came up behind her. She did not even turn to face him, but she was aware.

"What news do you bring me?" She spoke in a stern controlling voice.

"How did you know?" He whispered.

"I know everything. I am to be this land's new ruler. It would not pay for me to be so weak as to have someone be able to sneak up and take me by surprise." She growled at him.

"I was not trying to sneak up on you. I simply did not want to disturb you." He said continuing to bow.

"Stand up straight and tell me why you came here. I do not have time for this foolishness."

"Yes, my Queen, I have found them."

"You mean the boy and the others he travels with." She spun around to face him.

"Yes, they are nearing. As you predicted, they are coming in your direction. Though I do not quite know why." The Wraith questioned the intelligence of the situation.

"Oh, that is easy, I planted a vision in the girls head. She used the boy to collect information, and I simply gave her a bit more than she was looking for. I am pleased she took the bait, and when they arrive…I have a few more surprises for them."

"My Queen, may I ask…why do you want them?" The Wraith drew back in fear of being too forward with her.

"My reasons are my own, and not for you to question. Let's just say…the boy…I want for private reasons. The other two are quite different. They are powerful and not of the Dream Land. They are from a much higher realm, a place of great power. They could tear this place apart. That is why I want them gone. …. And if it brings me great power to destroy them." She began to laugh, she reveled in the idea of gaining more power.

"Very good my queen. What do you wish of me now?" He asked

"For now, just follow them, and observe. Make sure they are on the path here. If they stray, give them a nudge." She laughed

"Forgive my ignorance, but what do you consider a nudge?"

"Anything that gets them here alive. I never said they could not be damaged," A sinister smile crossed her face as she turned away from the wraith and considered her future. She craved whatever she could steal from Daniel and Jen would assure her rule of Dream Land forever.

"Oh, Wraith…" She called out to him as he started to leave.

"Yes, my Queen."

Maybe sending them through their own nightmares might make them move a little faster. Dig into the blond boy's memories. He and the girl were human once. I glimpsed into their past. Most of who they are together, came from a cemetery. The end result was a battle with a powerful demon. I'd start there, if I were you. The girl died in that battle. I am sure her fear is still deep within her. Maybe turning it lose will change the dynamic."

"Yes, my Queen. I know what to do." The Wraith acknowledged her as he turned and made his way out of the garden. As he returned to the open field where Jen and Daniel healed Zach, the wraith watched. He had to be right on his timing to catch them off guard.

He waited until the evening, and exhaustion overtook them all. Jen faded off to sleep first and soon Daniel followed. As the wraith approached, he spread his torn black robes and wrapped around them both. Jan and Daniel were transported back to the cemetery where they met. Neither one was aware they had fallen into the trap.

Mullins

Chapter Eighteen

The Dark Side of The Cemetery

Jen woke up confused. She looked around her. She was back in the mausoleum. She took a deep breath as she stood up. The place was still so familiar to her, even though she had not been there for over a year. She ran to the wall, to the right of the door. It was still there. The picture of Daniel, just like when she hid in the mausoleum to escape the gang.

She ran to the door and looked out. It was all there, her old home and the neighborhood. Everything as it should be. And things as they should not be. "This isn't right. My house caught fire when the gang broke in. The one in front of me, is as it was before I left." Jen felt her heart beat faster as she wondered what happened to Daniel. Had this all been a dream?

She turned to go back in. None of this made sense. As she sat upon the old stone bench, as she had so many times in the past, she called out Daniel's name. She didn't expect and answer, and she did not get one. She ran it all over in her mind. They had been travelling in Dream Land. She could not be there in her past.

She became angry and stood up to scream, and then it dawned on her. She was not the girl who came there as a victim so long ago. She was stronger, and since then she had become a White Lighter.

As she looked back towards the door, she remembered the house where she and Daniel spent so much time. In her mind, she called out to the place and prepared to orb. She channeled her energy and set it free to form….and then nothing.

She was beyond mad; this was not new to her. She had been trained by the best. She called for

Daniel again, pleading for him to appear. When nothing happened, she settled down and felt the reality of the grim quiet space where she was surrounded by the dead.

Jen was no longer scared of death. She was when she was a little girl, but her grandmother explained to her that the dead could not hurt you. As she grew up, she became stronger. After meeting Daniel and the spirits of the cemetery, she grew accustomed to their presence.

As she glanced around, she noticed that there were no dead anywhere she looked. It didn't seem right, they were always seeking her out, to deliver a message to a loved one or deal with unfinished business. She was like some kind of ghost counselor or medium.

As she thought about it, she felt a lot like the way she was when she came to the cemetery. No powers or abilities. Just a scared girl who did not know which way to turn. She had outgrown this.

She knew that much, and so did Daniel, but an outsider looking in would not.

She knew it now; she had been placed back into a memory of herself. This is why she could not call for Daniel. He was not there. This was a dream state, she was a Dream Walker with no abilities and no connection to the outside world. If she was stuck in this place, then Daniel may have been transported to his own memory.

Now, she knew she had an advantage. She knew more about this place, than anyone looking in from the outside. She had already lived and died in this place, and she did not plan on reliving her death again.

Making her way out of the mausoleum, she climbed the back steps of the house next door. Quickly, she made her way across the back porch and turned the knob. It was open just like before. Inside she was surrounded by memories, it was where she and Daniel hid before he was taken. And the place he returned to, when he escaped from the light.

As her mind raced over all the things she had forgotten in the year since she left, she realized the place had its good moments. If it were not for Daniel, she would not have grown to be the person she was that day. He gave her life again and a purpose, and for that, she had the willpower to fight her way out. Whoever put her in this dream, did it to scare and break her. What they did not take into account was, her desire to live.

Jen went out to the center of the cemetery. It was there, she saw the huge dam. This was the place she died. In her mind she flashed on it once more. The figures took life before her, as she watched her death re-enacted

Jen watched herself as she became frantic. She had to get to Daniel. As she ran for the open area to try to spot him, the demon Abraxas watched her. "And now my dear, it is your turn. I said I would have you. And now I will."

As the demon walked towards Jen, he commanded the water flow to increase from the bottom of the overflowing lake. As Jen ran, the water flowed faster in her direction and she was unaware, until she saw the wall approaching her. It was too late to get away. The water hit her hard and lifted her from the ground and flipped her limp body into the lower flooded area.

Jen struggled to get above the water as it swirled about her. She couldn't breathe. She tried to scream for help, but her mouth only filled with the muddy dirt filled water. Jen managed to get above the water level and spit up what she had taken in. She tried to scream but no one heard her. Taking a deep breath, she swam as hard as she could.

Abraxas watched her in amusement. "Perhaps I made it too easy for you." He spit forth, as he drove more water down the hill. With the wave came caskets and tombstones which were ripped up and beat against each other breaking them into small projectiles.

As Jen struggled to stay above water, the next wave hit her. The pieces of tombstones flew into the water all around her like bullets from a high-powered rifle. One piece hit Jen's shoulder, ripping the flesh open to a point, she had to stop and hold tight to it. As she looked away, she did not see the coffins flying down the hillside in the waters flow. As they scattered into the flooded area, the lids came open, and the dead emerged from the water all around her.

Jen turned to scream as she saw the rotted corpses. She struggled to get away as they moved closer to her. Like animated puppets, they reached out and grabbed hold of her. They held tight to her and prevented her from swimming, as she sank deep into the water. Jen let out one last fatal scream as they drug her into the deep abyss.

Abraxas stood just out the way. "I told you I would have you, now I do." He laughed as he turned his attention back to the battle.

Jen let out a muffled scream, as she knew in that moment, she had died. Her heart beat loudly in her chest, she had to find her way out of the dream.

Mullins

Chapter Nineteen

Death, Then Life, Then Death Again

Daniel felt himself orbing, but he did not know where. He tried to stop the event. As he forced his energy to tear apart the orb, he flew through the air and landed on the front yard. He was home again, but how could it be; this was a time where he was alive. He had traveled sixty years back in time. He listened, as he heard the screaming coming from the house. He knew this too well; it was the night he died.

"Mom why are you being so crazy about this? I just want to know the truth." Daniel pleaded with Emily, but she became outraged. The final threads of the lie she and her husband had hidden for sixteen years was unraveling. Daniel had stumbled onto the truth. Being a head strong teenager meant he was not going to give up easy and let it rest.

"Daniel, sometimes the past, is better left in the past. Why won't you just leave this all alone before you cause more problems than ever imagined." Emily pleaded with him.

"No, I want the truth. Is the woman I saw with dad, my mother, or are you. I am tired of being lied to. I have felt my whole life something was wrong. I don't know how, but I have always known, didn't you see how as a child I would never call you Mommy? Damn-it tell me the truth."

"Ok, you want the truth, then I will give it to you. You are not my son. You are the bastard child of my husband and his secretary. While I was home being the loving and devoted wife, your dad was out screwing around. He thought he wouldn't get caught. Well guess what, when you get another woman pregnant, then you get caught. At least my children will be born into a house of marriage." Emily spewed forth all the hatred she had pushed down for so long.

She reveled in delight as she unloaded years of pain and hatred. She never thought about the fact it was aimed at the wrong person. Emily's husband should have been her target, instead of an innocent sixteen-year-old boy bore the load of his father's sin.

Daniel stared on in disbelief as he tried to conceive how such a thing could be true. The man he had loved and respected his whole life, had been living a lie. And what was worse, he had made Daniel live that lie as well. His whole world began to crash around him. Nothing and no one he ever believed in was real anymore. They were just a group of actors, each one playing the roles they assigned themselves.

A tear ran down Daniel's face, as he looked into Emily's eyes. She was as much a victim as he was. Confusion filled his mind as he searched for any clear way to accept any of it. All he knew was, that he wanted to get out of the house of lies that was closing in around him. He turned and headed for the door, as a look of terror crept across Emily's face. Her only thought was. 'What have I done?'

Daniel raced for the door before Emily could plead with him not to go. She knew what she had done was wrong. She knew when James came home from work, there would be hell to pay for this. She had to fix it. She had to keep Daniel at home and persuade him not to tell his father what he found out.

Emily raced for the door and grabbed her keys. Daniel had to be nearby, there wasn't enough time for him to get far. As Emily raised the garage door, the rain poured on her head. She worked quickly to get down the drive, but in her confusion, she backed the car into the side porch before squealing tires and heading for the main road.

As she drove, the rain pelted her windshield. The old wipers were too shredded to keet the window clear. Emily could barely see as the tears burned her eyes and the windshield started to fog over. As she rounded the corner. She didn't see Daniel walking by the road. As she tried to wipe the windshield, the car swerved towards the edge of the road.

As Daniel heard the sound of the car coming at him, it was too late to move. He looked into the headlights bright white glow as the car ran him down. As he fell to the ground unconscious, his last thoughts were almost humorous. He started life as an accident and now he would die that same way.

Emily jumped from the car and ran to his side. Time stopped for her in that moment. Everything around her froze as she felt the pain hit her heart so hard it was going to explode. She screamed out for help, hoping someone, anyone would hear her. Emily just sat there in her frozen state cradling Daniel in her arms. The neighbors came as did the police, but Emily didn't even acknowledge them. She only whispered in Daniel's ear, "I am so sorry…I was wrong"

Daniel watched as his lifeless body was taken away. The pain was too much for him, as tears ran from his face. This was the first time he died. A Short time later, he woke up in the cemetery. He began a new life, one in which he met Jen. One which led him to the opportunity to live again.

He watched and waited the battle within the light, and the Shadow creatures who came after him after he escaped. This version was close to his reality, but small pieces seemed to be missing or changed. Daniel watched intently looking for more mistakes.

Shaking his head, he knew this was all engineered, because events that were to come were not right. Missing were the events of when he entered the light and fought to live again. Jen did not even see that. Daniel was alone then. Whoever was calling the shots here did not know all the facts. Daniel was stuck in a dream and he knew it, he would fight his way out.

Chapter Twenty

Dreams and Nightmares

The Wraith stood over the still bodies of Jen and Daniel. To anyone else, they appeared to be dead, but in Dream Land, they were merely Dream Walkers. Their bodies lay upon the ground as their minds were off in a different place, living out dream and nightmares.

The Wraith looked content with what he had accomplished. His queen would be pleased with him. As he looked down upon his victims, he watched the stories playing out in their minds. He had done well in choosing events that would affect them emotionally. He hoped that reliving the past would cripple them. If not completely, then the separation of the two would do damage as well.

Zach's healing was nearly complete, he felt groggy, but better than he was. He tilted his head from side to side before he opened his eyes and say the wraith standing before him. He began to open his mouth to scream but caught himself as he saw Jen and Daniel unconscious on the ground before him.

Zach watched and studied the Wraith's movements. He had to find a way to free them from the Wraith's control. He had no way to stop a Wraith, and no abilities to fight it. All he had was a bag of sand. And with that thought, he began to smile.

His memory was clear now. He could recall all the times he was forced into dreamland with the sand. If it could control him and send him places, then it had to be able to bring someone back.

The sand had been used, and barely half the pouch remained. He had to be sure of how it would work. As he ran his fingers through the sand, his vision changed. Before his eyes were glimpses of Daniel and Jen, both in the same cemetery but in different times.

When Daniel arrived in the cemetery, Jen had not been born. Zach kept watching the visions, they were in the same place. Time was the issue. They had to be brought to the same place and time. They could work together at that point.

The wraith was the real issue Zach had to deal with, he had to distract him and get him away long enough to spread the sand on them. Zach watched the visions, and tried to send a message to both dreams but he lacked experience and ability.

Beside him on the ground were many stones varying in size. He did not know if a Wraith was capable of feeling pain, but perhaps now was the time to find out. Zach picked up two of the larger stones and hurled them at the Wraiths head and upper body.

The stones found their mark, hitting exactly where they were meant to. The creature fell to the side. Zach was sure then; they could feel pain. He would remember that, as he leapt to his feet and hurled several more stones. The Wraith was down, but Zach did not know for how long. He would have to work Quickly.

He reached into his pouch and grabbed a handful of sand and stood over his friends. As he scattered the sand, he focused his energy on both dreams. Inside he saw Daniel and Jen. He did not know how to put them in the same spot, but he did know how to open a doorway between and allow one of them to cross.

As the sand sank into the dreams, a rift began to open just inside the mausoleum. Zach called out to both dreams trying to implant a subtle message. He did not know if they would hear him, but he tried in the little amount of time he had.

As his message rang through the dream state, the Wraith began to stir. Zach watched as the creature rose back into the air. As it turned towards him, Zach backed up a step at a time. He had nowhere to go. His only hope, would be either Jen or Daniel would wake up.

Chapter Twenty-One

A Dream Is

Jen looked around the cemetery that was once home to her. It looked the same but there was so much missing. As she looked at the stones and walked back towards the house, she was sure this place was a nightmare reminder. When she was younger, she would have fallen apart if faced with half as much pain. She was stronger now.

"I don't know who is responsible for this, but be warned, it is not working. I will get out of here, and when I come for you. You will pay so dearly for what you have done." Jen called out.

As she reached the back steps of the house, she found her way to the corner of the porch and sat down. She tried to clear her head and figure out any way she could use her abilities to get out. "Daniel would know what to do." She whispered.

As the silence of her surroundings closed in on her, she heard a familiar sound. It was a scooter, making its nightly rounds of the cemetery. She remembered it well, and the large man who rode it. Larry had come to mean so much to her when she was alone there. She sat back and watched the vision unfold. She had not seen him in so long. She felt tears forming as she remembered him and his death.

Jen moved to a location out of the way so she would not interfere with what was about to occur. The scooter was soothing to her and as she watched Larry come into view, she relived her first encounter, as she hid from him after breaking into the cemetery at night. She watched herself run in fear of being caught that night.

In the relived event, as Jen tried to work up the nerve to move, there was a weird noise in the distance. Jen couldn't quite make it out but it sounded mechanical. As she focused on the sound, it got closer and closer. The sound was like a mechanical engine. She tried to determine what direction it was coming from. As the sound got louder, she looked around the cemetery road ways and saw a light headed right for her. She thought to herself that maybe hiding in a cemetery was not a good idea after all.

The sound was louder now and the light shined in her direction. Her heart sank in her chest, she was sure she was caught, by whoever or whatever it was.

Jen didn't know what to do. If she ran, she would be seen, and if she stayed, she most certainly would be found. She decided the best thing to do was stay curled up behind the bushes and see what happened. The noise was right behind her and the light lit up the whole area where she was hiding. She looked through the bushes and saw what was coming, and to her amazement, her fear faded immediately. It was a short fat man on a motor scooter. She almost laughed at how comical the man looked. In her mind, he kind of looked like a circus clown. At once she realized he was not coming for her, but making rounds on the road behind her.

The little scooter turned the corner beside her and moved away. As soon as he was out of sight, she laughed. How could she have panicked so much over a fat guy on a scooter? And then she thought, maybe this was what she needed, to convince herself that she was safe. Her fear was gone now and a weird sense of calm filled her.

Jen smiled as she enjoyed the memory and her sense of calm. Once again, she had reclaimed a bit of the feeling she needed. "But what do I do now? I can't stay here forever." As Jen laughed at herself, she remembered she used to talk to herself a lot before Daniel came along.

As she finished her thought, a sound emerged. It was a boy's voice. She spun around looking for the source, but she was all alone. Then it came again, this time she heard it clearly, "Find the rift between your dreams." She knew who it was now, Zach was trying to send them help. Trouble was, she had no idea how to find a rift in a dream. She hoped that Daniel would understand and come for her.

Mullins

Chapter Twenty-Two

A Wish Your Heart Makes

Daniel paced back and forth, trying to figure out how to escape the dream state he had been sealed in. He was sure the answer to his escape would lie within the cemetery. So much of his life after death seemed to revolve around it. As he headed down the deserted street towards the main gate, the darkness of the night enveloped him,

There was an eerie deadly feel as he crossed the main gate. In this version of the cemetery, there was no one there to greet him, not the dead or the living. The feel made Daniel uncomfortable. There had never been a time, that he walked through the cemetery, that a spirit was not there to greet him.

He thought about it and decided that he preferred the dead to nothing at all. With them, there was always someone to talk to. But this world wasn't real, was it? This world was made up by someone who dabbled in his and Jen's brains. That made him feel violated.

As Daniel grew closer to the street to the mausoleum, he felt all the familiar things come back to him. It was strange, but he missed this place. He even found himself missing the mausoleum he had been entombed in. He hadn't thought about it much since he and Jen left the cemetery. He thought that he hated the place after Jen died there.

His life had been a crazy one, then his death even more crazy. That was until he found Jen. They had a strange connection before he came back to life. Neither one questioned it. They just accepted everything that happened, and moved on when they both became White-Lighters.

As Daniel approached the door to the mausoleum, he reached for the handle. Almost intimidated, he turned it and stepped in. He had the old feeling that Jen would be there inside waiting for him. Whenever they had to find each other, they went there. Both for different reasons.

Daniel walked inside and to the left. He had been there so many times. The tomb with his picture on it, was there like so many times he had seen it before. He reached out to touch the picture. He experienced a shiver as his fingers touched the stone around the picture.

In his mind, he knew his dead body was inside the enclosure. In a way there were two versions of him. The body he was born with resided within. Then there was the body he was given by Angels, when he was allowed to return from the dead. He felt sad for his original body. Then from within, came a deep emotion, "No, this is not real and not the time. I dealt with this so long ago."

As he turned and looked away, he saw the generations of his family that had been there for over a hundred years. There was his father across the way, and the woman who he had thought was his mother. He sighed as he turned around and his eyes focused on the spot where Jen's body had been placed. He held back the pain he had buried so far down inside himself for so long.

As he felt the tears in his eyes welling, he heard and echoing sound. It started out low and then grew louder. As it reached its loudest tone, Daniel recognized the voice. Zach had managed to find him. He left Daniel with the same words that Jen had heard.

Daniel shook his head as he looked around. "How the hell do you find a rift? I can't see anything." Daniel's anger rose, as he now knew he had a way out and it was hidden from him. He turned to try to light the room with his orb light, but nothing happened. Then he realized, this time in his life, he had no abilities. He had only just died. At that point he couldn't even orb.

He paced as he spoke out loud, "Jen, I wish you could hear me. I don't know how to get to you. I can't even rescue you. I am powerless here in this dream."

He walked over to the back stone wall of the structure. He had appeared there so many times, when he and Jen first came together. His bright blue light filled the enclosure as he stepped out of the orb.

He reached his hand and ran his fingers over the stone. At the same time in Jen's dream, she reached for the same point on the wall. She breathed deep as she was sure she felt Daniel's presence.

As their finger's touched the same spot at the same time, the rift opened. A light shot forth, and they both smiled. They had found a way to each other. "Jen, if you can hear me, step back!" Daniel screamed through to her. Jen moved back as Daniel through himself against the wall.

The light grew brighter and Jen flashed on her memories of Daniel. He had come to her again. As he flew through the void, he tripped and landed at her feet. His body shook back and forth for a moment, as he felt his energy surge through his body again.

Jen fell to her knees and hugged his neck. "You came back to me." She said laughing.

"I promised I would always find you. Just took me a minute this time." He said smiling at her.

"Yeah, so how do we get out of here? I have my powers, but everything here is screwing with them." Jen raised a hand and tried to make a fireball, as she threw it, the whole place lit up, as it missed its mark.

"Well, at least you had powers, where I was, I had nothing. I couldn't even orb." Daniel mocked her. "I don't know, maybe together, we change the way things work here. What I do know, is we have to get back to Zach before the Wraith takes him.

Chapter Twenty-Three

When You Are Fast Asleep

Walking back and forth, neither of them had an idea of how to escape the dream prison. If it was a simple battle of the dead to stay alive, they had all the answers. Jen put her hands to her head, and pulled back her long brown hair trying to get a bit of air. The mausoleum had become stuffy.

"Jen, what would you say was the worst battle we fought here."

"Oh, I don't know. Maybe the one where the demons killed me." She snapped at Daniel.

"I wasn't trying to make you angry; I was just wondering if that would be the place of the most energy."

'What of it? Wait, could we channel the energy and supercharge a single orb out of here?" She began to get excited.

"Well yes, theoretically. At least I hope I am correct." Daniel stumbled over his idea.

"And if you are wrong?" Jen asked.

"We end up in a reconstructed demonic battle that we had our asses kicked in." He answered.

"Yeah, but we eventually won the battle…with a few deaths along the way." Jen spoke up before realizing one of the deaths was her own.

"I don't want to lose you again." Daniel said as he put his hand on her shoulder.

"This time we stay together. You only died because we were separated."

"Agreed, now we only have to get to the right time in this dream for the battle to begin."

"I think we can manipulate the dream and orb to the right time. My only concern is running into ourselves. We cannot occupy the same space as them for long. We need to orb there and jump into the timeline quickly." Daniel explained.

"Will that happen? We are in a dream, not the real timeline." Jen was confused.

When I was trapped in the other dream, I watched myself die. I was there at the same time the other me was. I saw him get run down by the car."

"Point taken; we cannot get in the way of ourselves. They cannot see us; we cannot see them."

"Take my hand and focus on the day of the battle where you died. At that time, I was tied to the stone cross, and you had tried to come for me when you saw Abraxas."

As they held hands, the light began to surround them. A swirling white light came from within Jen and a bright blue came from Daniel. As the light swirled it mixed together and they became one. Outside the light, time progressed. Minutes turned to hours, then hours to days, until they reached their time destination.

Stepping outside of the mausoleum, they turned the corner to see the blasts of light filling the sky. In a way, it was beautiful, but in truth it was deadly, as within the battle, the light meant death on both sides.

Daniel grabbed hard to Jen's hand as he looked up at the old house. From the doorway, the dream's timeline started and Jen and her friend Abigail ran from the door. As Jen fell backwards, she stared at herself running up the hill.

She turned to Daniel with an angered look. "Does my hair really look like that?"

"You have to be kidding me. Just come on, we are a bit early, but maybe we can get to where we need to be." Daniel was serious now; this was all too real to him.

They ran along in the distance, hiding from everyone in the battle. From just above the hill, Daniel saw the fatal arrow that killed Abigail. He breathed deep from his pain for his friend, even though he knew this was just a reconstructed dream.

As they made their way to the rear of the battle, they waited for the moment when Jen reentered the scene. Daniel was sure this was the perfect time; she had just come back to life and she was angry.

As the dream version of Jen appeared, they watched themselves from the back of the tree line. Jen stepped out of the light as she orbed into the cemetery. Coming in just near the lake, she looked over to the hill, where the water had washed her down. On the hillside there were still the coffins and the remains if dead body parts. She felt her body tremble in anger, as she turned to walk up the hill.

As she arrived at the top, she looked over to see Daniel tied to the stone cross. She smiled as she mentally sent him the message, "I'm coming." She moved closer, and watched as the fighting there was intense. As she entered the open area, she saw Abraxas who was walking over to Daniel. She was not aware if he knew of her presence, but she wanted the element of surprise.

As the demon prepared to strike Daniel again to wake him up, Jen came up from behind. "Get the hell away from him you bastard." Jen walked quickly up to him. The demon was surprised by her appearance, he still believed she was dead. As he looked at her in disbelief, he raised his hand to strike at her. Jen levitated out of his reach; his arm flew past her.

"What game is this?" He asked.

"It's no game. I've come for Daniel. I suggest you get out of my way."

The demon laughed at her as he turned away. "What can you do? You are a puny human."

Jen felt the power building within her. As she threw her arms outward, she floated higher and her body began to glow a bright white light. The demon turned and looked up in fear as he realized Jen was more of a threat than he ever imagined.

As he began to run, Jen unleashed her full power upon him. As the light penetrated his form, he raised up into the air. As he shook, his body was being torn apart at a molecular level. With one final wave of power Jen scattered his body all around the cemetery.

Landing at his feet, Jen reached up and freed Daniel's arm's one at a time. Pulling him close, he buried his head in her shoulder. As Jen held him, she formed a yellow light around him, that healed and brought him back to full power again.

"I got to save you for once." She laughed at him.

"Yeah, about that, how did you do this?"

"I am a fast learner I guess."

"We have to get the light open. I think I know how to do it." Daniel said as he studied the source of the blockage.

Rising up into the air, Daniel spun around in a circle. The flashing of the blasts in the area reflected on the skin of his chest as he spun faster. As he threw out his arms and then aimed them upwards, a blast of light stronger than he had ever emitted flew straight into where the light should have been. The power shook the ground around the cemetery, as the dark figures that clung to the light fell one by one, disintegrating as they plummeted to the earth below.

Back at the tree line, Daniel grabbed Jen's hand. "This is it. This place has absorbed so much power. We just have to add our own to it and get out of here."

Daniel pulled at Jen as they arrived just behind the battle scene. He took both her hands, and they once again formed their orb, as they channeled the energy that surrounded them. A blinding light formed around them, as they lifted into the air and their forms began to become light. A wormhole appeared and they flew outside the dream finding their way back to Dream Land.

As they emerged from the light, they returned to their bodies. Daniel opened his eyes, as the Wraith approached Zach. Raising his hands, a bright powerful charge flew from within him. The Wraith began to disintegrate before them, as Jen walked up from behind.

"I think I have had just about enough of you." She said, as her face began to turn read and she raised her arms. She shook as she blasted her energy forward. "I don't think he will be bothering anyone again."

As she turned and walked off in the distance, Zach came over to Daniel. "Is she always like that?"

"Nah, sometimes she really gets mad. You should be around for that." Daniel said laughing.

"I think we still need to talk about what you two are." Zach could not withhold his curiosity.

"You could call us White Lighters, or if you prefer…Angels."

Mullins

Chapter Twenty-Four

Return of the Sandman

The three travelers once again joined together, to return to their original quest. Each had recovered from their own trials. Zach's health was returned and he seemed more energetic than ever. Daniel remained a bit moody from his death experience. He still struggled to understand how his life could come to an end. Jen shook it all off, in her true fashion. She was no longer the abandoned girl whose family left her behind as she had to take refuge in a cemetery. She was becoming a woman of power.

As they collected themselves and started to walk away, a golden light filled the space behind them. It was a Sandman's doorway, taking shape and full form. Daniel spun around not knowing what to expect as a young girl flew forward out of the opening.

Looking up at the three people in front of her, she almost screamed. "Please back off. I am not a threat." She blasted out loudly.

"Who are you?" Daniel demanded an answer.

"I am Lacey. I am a Sandman. Just not one of the evil ones."

"What do you mean evil ones." Jen stepped forward questioning her.

"Look, I don't have time for all this, there is a Sandman coming up behind me. He has been chasing me for days. He did some really bad things on the Earth Plane. He over dosed a woman with sand. I caught him, and he chased me into the doorway. I have been running ever since. He wants to kill me." She explained.

"This woman, do you know who she was?" Zach asked, stepping forward to be seen.

"Yes, Zach, it was your mother. I have seen you before, many times. You have been trained as a Sandman. You probably do not remember it all.

You have had your memories tampered with." She explained.

"Yes, my memories were hidden, but now they have been returned. Why would you Sand People try to use me since I was a child?" He asked

"I had no part of it. I am only 15, this was going on long before I was recruited. The Sandman group has been dwindling over the years. Mostly because of the separation from within. Some of the Sandmen want to form a powerful but evil group set on controlling dream to achieve their goals. I am not one of them. Sadly, there are few of us left that are on the side of good." She said as she looked back to watch the doorway.

She watched intently, as the doorway began to tremble. She knew then someone was nearing the portal to reenter Dream Land. She turned towards them and gave a terrified look. She knew her time was almost over.

"What is it?" Daniel asked.

"He's here, and I don't have the power to stop him. He will kill me!" Her voice trailed off.

"No, we will protect you." Zach tried to reassure her.

Jen stepped forward. "Hold on guys, we know nothing of this situation. Hang back." Walking forward to the girl, Jen placed a hand on the girl's shoulder, and a flash of memories filled her head. Jen read through the last days of the girl. She had been telling the truth for the most part, but there was so much more going on that she did not tell.

Jen removed her hand and turned to Daniel. He could read Jen's expression, there was concern. It was not all good. "It's Ok, she is not lying about being chased. He does plan to kill her. I read her future. If we do not intervene, she will die." Jen said as she moved closer to Daniel.

"What aren't you telling us?" he whispered as she came to his side. "We need to talk when we are alone. It is worse than we ever imagined. The Sandmen have a new mission in life."

As Jen turned back to the doorway, the light from within surged and a form took shape. The Sandman flew forward and landed beside Lacey. She pulled back and prepared to run as he grabbed hold of her.

"Now, now, little one, you aren't going anywhere. I have you. Prepare for your end."

"No, I don't think that will be happening today." Jen commanded as she stepped forward.

"Who the hell do you think you are?" The Sandman Adam asked.

"Oh, I am your worst nightmare." Jen said laughing. "Now, let her go."

"Hmm, I am going to let her go for a few puny humans?" His smugness radiated through his words.

"You should never underestimate three people you have never met before. We are so much more than just humans." Daniel spoke out confidently.

As Daniel looked on to the Sandman, inside he began to charge his power. Turning his head to

Jen, she knew the message he was giving her. She too prepared for the fight. The Sandman looked at them, as his goggles engaged, and within a computer screen lit up where only he could see.

He scanned Daniel and then one by one the others. Adam read the information provided about White Lighters. He knew he had no way to win this fight. Rather than run away, he was willing to. His only thought was to go out a hero to his cause. A smile crossed his lips as he grabbed into his bag for a huge handful of sand.

Chapter Twenty-Five

Sacrifice for The Uprising

As The Sandman pulled his hand out of the bag and prepared to throw the sand, Daniel pushed Lacey out of the way. Zach grabbed her arm and pulled her to safety out of reach of the flying sand. As she fell into Zach, she looked up at him as she was worshiping a hero.

Daniel and Jen stood strong, as they let loose the power they had been holding back. A mixture of light flew forward dissolving the sand that was thrown at them. As their power light moved forward, it met with the Sandman's skin. He stood strong as the layers of his skin beginning to burn away bit by bit.

He yelled out with a mix of pain and relief as he felt his body being torn apart all the way down until his bones shattered. It was over, far faster than anyone could have imagined. Not much remained to fall to the ground. When it was all done, there was mostly a pile of sand where his bag fell.

Jen looked at the remains in disappointment. "I hate to do things like this. I never wanted to be a White Lighter to kill. I only wanted to help those who needed me. Seems I do that too little."

"You are just doing what you have to. He would have killed an innocent if you had not intervened." Daniel tried to reassure her.

"Not so innocent as you would think. There is something going on here that is so much more than we ever expected. The Sandmen are splitting for a reason. The group itself is reforming into a militia." Jen explained.

"You mean militia like a fighting group?' Daniel asked.

"No, I mean militia, like Nazi storm troopers, just without Hitler. They want to dominate and take over the Earth Realm. They are developing weapons of mass destruction and control. Sand is the least of their arsenal."

"Are you totally sure you saw all that. Could you have read her imagination?" Daniel asked.

"Daniel, I am never wrong. That girl could easily be one of Hitler's Youth Group. And it is worse, they are readying the coronation of a new Queen who will lead them." Jen was angered by the who concept.

"Can we stop them? Is there any way we can stop this from happening?"

"There are too many of them. Too many to focus on. We have to get to their Queen. If no one leads, then that may slow them down until all of them can be controlled." Jen responded.

"What part does Lacey play in all of this?" Daniel asked.

"She is not all bad, I think just a little brainwashed. I would be careful of as much as she knows of our plans. And the real problem is right before us." Jen said as she directed Daniel to look towards Zach, who was becoming enthralled with the young girl.

Jen walked over and took Zach's arm, pulling him away as she said, "Excuse us please."

Lacey looked on in confusion, as Jen led Zach out of the girl's range. "We have a problem." Jen whispered.

"What is going on? I don't understand. It is all taken care of, right?" Zach was confused.

"Not really, I read your new girlfriend. She had secrets and they are not good. The Sandmen are about to go to war, and your girlfriend believes in the cause. They want to cross over and control the Earth Realm." Jen looked him in the eye as she awaited his reaction.

Zach looked down and considered what he had heard, and realized how foolish he had been to trust someone he had just met. He had let his guard down for a pretty face. He looked up at his friends, "I am sorry. I know better than to just trust someone.

After all that has been done to me, trust should be a bigger issue. How do we handle this?"

"We keep tight lipped, and let her slip up and tell us all she knows. She has been on the inside of this crazy group. I bet she knows way more than I could read off of her in one setting. She will eventually expose herself if she is good or bad. Then we deal with her in any way we have to." Jen wished she had not seen all that she did.

Mullins

Chapter Twenty-Six

A Stranger in the Fellowship

As they began to leave, the golden doorway dissolved in front of them. Zach watched intently before falling to his knees and opening his sand bag. He gathered the dead Sandman's remaining sand as fast as he could.

Lacey came up beside him. "Why are you doing that?"

"My bag is almost replenished. I might need this later. We need all the defenses we can come up with." Zach continued in claiming the sand as she moved back.

"Why would you need the sand? No human can use sand, they do not have the control to wield it. Unless you are more than you seem…"

"It's a long story and one I do not care to share right now. So, if you don't mind, I would like to finish this."

Lacey walked away, glancing back to him from time to time. She reached up to pull down her goggles and glanced in his direction. The computer within flashed lights and on the screen a two-word description blinked…Sandman.

Lacey knew his history, Zach was human. She did not understand how he could be identified as a Sandman. She slipped the goggles back to the top of her head as she stared on in confusion.

Zach finished his task and joined the others, as they began to walk towards the mountain ahead. The silence was deadly, it was if no one wanted to share any secrets and the silence weaved around all of them.

As they began their entrance to the mountain range, Jen finally broke the silence. "Would someone say something? I cannot take the silence; you are all driving me crazy."

"Ok, I will start." Lacey interjected. "How is it that Zach is a Sandman? He was never supposed to be one. And why are you all giving me the silent treatment. I did nothing wrong but ask for help."

"We never said you did anything wrong. We are only being guarded." Daniel replied.

"Guarded? I have never been a threat to you." Lacey became angry.

Jen moved in closer and tried to find the right words. "I am an empath. When I touched your arm, I read your history and saw your life. We know about the Sandmen, and how they are preparing for war. You were a part of that."

"No, I am not, I have been observing what is going on. To do that, I had to pretend to go along with their ways. I never believed in their cause. If you do not believe me, read me again."

Jen reached out to her and took hold. She traveled through the memories more slowly and explored what she had already seen in flashes. Lacey was not on the side of the storm troopers, but still Jen felt there was something that was being withheld. She could not locate the part that was being hidden from them.

"Now, did you find what you were looking for." Lacey probed her.

"I found some of what you said to be true. Still underneath it all, you are hiding something, and for you to be able to do that means you are very good. No 15-year-old girl is that good at defying my search. So, do I trust you…not so much." Jen said in an authoritative tone. "Oh, and by the way, I am just a few years older than you, there is way too much in your history for your age. Just saying."

"Are you trying to say something to me?" Lacey snapped at her.

"No, not trying to say anything, I think I just said it. I don't really trust you." Jen slapped back.

Jen walked to Daniel and Zach and stood strong by them. She was not about to back down. She wondered if assisting the girl to kill the Sandman was a mistake. She wondered if they had chosen the wrong one to save. It would not be the first time a fake innocent cried out for help. Jen did not like where all this was going, but she was sure they had to free themselves from the new member.

Mullins

Chapter Twenty-Seven

Into the Woods

Zach walked out to Lacey, as she stared at them in disbelief. "I know you may not have enough sand to get where you are going." He said as he reached in and grabbed a handful of sand and spread it into the air to form the doorway. "Now you can go wherever you need to. This time there is no Sandman on your heels trying to kill you."

"Zach, I promise, I am not evil. Please come with me, you do not belong with them. We are Sandmen. Come home with me." She tried to tempt him into leaving.

"I am not sure that is going to work on me. You see, my friends saved me and I most certainly belong with them. You however, are another story. Perhaps you should go ahead and enter the doorway."

Zach turned his back on her as she stepped inside. The light from within warped her form as she slid out of sight and the doorway closed in on itself. Daniel looked him in the eyes, and gave him a look of respect as they all closed in and headed into the tree line.

They climbed for what seemed like hours as they reached a peak to rest. Jen had been silent for so long. She had seen too much of the possible future and it worried her. The last thing she wanted was another battle. Too many friends had been lost that way.

As Daniel built a fire, Jen sat cross-legged on the ground. She folded her arms, and in an instant, entered a meditation state. Her mind connected with the Dream Land. She reached out far and wide. In this state, she could explore the Sandmen and their plans.

In her travels, she found Lacey and did the one thing she said she never would do. She took control of her long enough to experience the inside of the Sandman Collective. She could see all that Lacey did. She would be able to collect information first hand and not from a tainted memory of another.

Inside their compound, Jen watched as training sessions were going on. It felt as if they had become soldiers. They were trained in combat and warfare. Their jumpsuits now displayed new insignias with a design.

Jen looked on, as she walked along at the rows of soldiers lined up for inspection all with the same glowing red goggles lit from within. They were ready for war. This was not new; the movement had been coming for some time. The Earth Realm was in more danger than they had imagined.

As she continued to another part of the complex, she witnessed the new production of sand. No longer was it yellow gold in color. The new sand was laced with red. As she listened, she knew why. The new sand could be spread, not by individual, but by area. It could be spread by atmosphere deployment.

The new sand only had to touch a person's skin to be absorbed. Much like a neurotoxin, the new sand was as deadly as it needed to be. Jen took a deep breath as she turned to be face to face with another Sandman.

"You have been summoned by the new Queen." He said, as he turned to the side to allow her to pass.

Jen thanked him, as she walked forward. The Sandman guided her through the long hallways, to the hidden location the Queen had been sequestered in. As they reached the end of the hall, Jen was stopped and informed she would be called for, when the Queen was ready.

The wait seemed to take forever, as Jen fought to stay in control. Lacey was not as weak as she pretended to be, and she clawed at Jen to regain her control. Jen however was not giving up; this was the secret Lacey had hidden. Jen was not about to miss this, not for anything.

As the Sandman returned to escort Lacey to the Queen. Jen dug her heels in, and retained control. Lacey weakened and her control was out of grasp. She was led into the doorway to the secret chamber prepared to hide the monarchy.

"Come, Come tell me what you have learned." The Queen insisted.

Jen looked up at her as she fumbled for the right words. When the queen turned to look at her, she seemed frustrated. "What daughter of mine should have so much trouble finding her words? Now, I will ask again. What have you learned about this group?"

Jen just uttered the word, "Daughter?" Then she released control to Lacey. She now knew what she had came for. The secret that had been buried so deep in the girl was out. A smile came across the lips of Jen's face as she returned to her body.

Mullins

Chapter Twenty-Eight

Dirty Little Secrets

Jen shook as she returned from her out of body experience. As she regained her composure, she stood up too quickly. As Daniel caught Jen's arm, and prevented her falling, she took a deep breath. She had so much to tell him. But she didn't know where to begin.

"Wait, I do know where to begin. I was right!" She screamed.

"About what?" Daniel knew not to rush her, or they would be there for hours.

"Lacey! I knew she was hiding something. I was so right. One of these days I am going to learn to trust my empathy." She said pacing back and forth.

"Jen, what were you right about? What did she hide?" Daniel asked.

"She's not just a Sandman. She is also the new Queen's daughter."

"So, what does that mean?" Zach asked.

"It means, the new Queen plans to infiltrate the Earth Realm and enslave everyone there. I went to the complex they have set up. They are mass processing this red sand that can be sent by air. You breathe or touch this stuff and you are a zombie under their control." Jen tried to contain herself as she stressed the seriousness of what she had seen.

"That is so screwed up!" Zach blasted out.

"Yes, but how can we stop an army of Sandmen?" Daniel asked.

"We have to go inside the complex and slow them down until we can figure out what to do." Jen replied.

"Jen, can you guide us all there inside an orb, if I add my power to yours. I know it is three this time and you have never done that before." Daniel worried about the idea of putting too much strain on her.

"Maybe if I rest a while and prepare. What would happen if I lose it during orb?" She asked.

"We could all disintegrate or maybe slam into a wall when we reenter solid space." Daniel shrugged, as he tried to find the words to express his concern.

"What if Zach ads a little sand to our orbs?" Jen asked.

"We would supercharge our jump. We might have better control." Daniel answered, more hopeful than before.

"I am willing to do anything to help. We have to stop this. I have family and friends that I don't want to see hurt." Zach spoke like he understood the need to fight.

They gathered around and sorted out when they would leave. From within his pack, Daniel pulled out food and water. As they passed them around, the three formulated an entry point based on Jen's memory of the building.

In the area where they manufactured the red sand, there was a back hallway where no one seemed to travel since the machinery was shut down. That would have to be the orb point. If we hit it fast enough, no one should see us before we can study the machinery and try to stop the red sand distribution.

"I guess I am the weak link in all this." Zach said under in a quite grumble.

"What makes you think that?" Jen said as she cleared her throat.

"You guys are experienced and have lots of training with your abilities. It is obvious when you do anything. I have a bag of sand that I have barely clue about using. I mean sure, I am physically capable of fighting, but these guys can freeze me in my tracks. They have been doing it my whole life." Zach moaned.

"Well, I am no expert on Sandmen or their abilities, but maybe we could train you a little in what

we do know and get you a little more experienced."
Jen offered.

As they pulled from all the memories each
had of interacting with the Sandmen, Zach became
more exposed to using the sand bag and how the sand
could do more than just open a doorway. As the
hours passed, Zach became more confident. His
view changed from victim to someone who was
ready to fight back.

Mullins

Chapter Twenty-Nine

All Hail the Queen

The morning came quickly as the three prepared to orb to the complex. As they closed in to stand together, Jen stood in the front as Daniel and Zach stood behind her forming a pyramid shape.

Jen reached behind, as they all took hands. She formed a shield around them as her power rose. Daniel followed behind with his addition of power. Jen looked over her shoulder and smiled at Zach, "Now it's your turn. Let the sand fly."

Zach had sand in his right hand waiting for the call. As he threw it upwards, the whole area that was filled with light, took on a golden tone. Jen increased her energy as she yelled, "Hold on."

The light lifted them into the air as a wormhole formed around them and they were sucked inside. The three held tight to each other as they were bounced around the shimmering passage. "Daniel what's wrong with this orb, we are becoming unstable." Jen screamed over the rumbling of the light walls around them.

"Just hold it together, we will make it. I think it is just because there is more mass than usual." He answered.

Jen watched as she guided them to the end of the trip. She could see the opening in her mind as they slammed their way along. As the hall came closer, Jen could no longer hold on, and the protective shield disintegrated as they crashed into the wall of the hallway.

Jen rolled hard into a wall slamming her shoulder. Daniel managed to extend an energy wall in the last seconds to stop Zach and himself from crashing into each other. It was not a perfect landing, but they did survive the journey.

"Is everyone OK?" Daniel called out as they scrambled to their feet.

"Yes, I think." Zach called back.

"I think I might need a little help." Jen said as she struggled to get to her feet.

"Jen! You dislocated your shoulder." Daniel said as he ran over and put his hand over the area and it started to turn yellow. "How does that feel?" He asked.

"It hurts like a bitch, but I have had worse things done to me. Now, tell me, why did the orb break up like that?"

"I am beginning to think this place was protected by a shield or something. Doesn't matter now, we made it and we are all alive."

"Why is this place so quiet. I thought it would be like a factory?" Zach asked.

"You are right, it was noisy before. Something is different. Did we orb to the wrong place?" Jen said as she looked around. "No, this is the same place. There is the red sand." She said as she pointed towards the large vats that were filled to the tops.

"Where did they all go? Are they invading already?" Zach asked.

"No, if they were, the vats would be emptied." Daniel turned to Jen and made a face. "Can you get anything from touching one of their personal objects?"

"Yeah, I can, now that I can move my arm again." She said as she moved to a table where one of the Sandmen had left his goggles.

Jen grasped them in her hands and pulled the red lenses to her. The memories of the owner flew at her, like she was driving down a highway. She pushed away useless memories and ones she did not want to see. And then she saw the man put down his goggles as he prepared to leave for the queen's coronation.

"Their new queen is taking her crown today. I think we need to see this for ourselves." Jen insisted.

"Why would we want to see that?' Daniel asked "…and even if we did, how would we get in unseen."

Jen reached over to the wall where several uniforms hung. "Pick your size."

A short time after they were dressed, they followed the sound of the crowd outside moving down the hillside to the coronation gathering. Making their way through the crowd the came to the side of the elevated platform. It was there they saw Lacey, out of uniform and looking more like a queen's daughter. She did not notice them as they climbed the steps to get a better view.

The queen approached and prepared to receive her crown. She was covered in a sequined gown, and a veil that covered her face. She walked slowly and gracefully as she climbed one step at a time until she reached her throne.

As she turned to be seated, her daughter reached over to remove the veil, to show her face. The material fell softly from her skin, as she lit up with a smile and looked around to her gathered crowd. As she turned towards the three companions, Zach's stomach turned, as he felt as if he would throw up. He grabbed hard to Jen's hand as he stepped forward onto the stage and uttered one single word. "Mother!"

Continued in

Dream Walker Book Two:

Wide Awake In Dream Land

Thanks for choosing this book, if you enjoyed it, please leave positive feedback.

Included at the end of this book, are the first two chapters of G.W. Mullins' Best-Selling title Rise Of The Dark Lighter Book One – Dark Awakening

About the Author

G.W. Mullins is an Author, Photographer, and Entrepreneur of Native American / Cherokee descent. He has been a published author for over 10 years. His writing has focused on the paranormal and Native American studies. Mullins has released several books on the history/stories/fables of the Native American Indians.

Among his books are the extremely successful *Star People, Sky Gods, And Other Tales Of The Native American Indians*, *The Native American Story Book - Stories Of The American Indians For Children Volumes 1-5*, *The Native American Cookbook*, and *Walking With Spirits Native American Myths, Legends, And Folklore Volumes 1 Thru 6*.

He has released the complete series from his Sci/fi Fantasy Series *From The Dead Of Night*, including the Best-Selling titles - *Daniel Is Waiting*, and *Daniel Returns*.

His most recent work includes the new series *Rise Of The Snow Queen* featuring *Book One The Polar Bear King*, and *Book Two The War Of The Witches*. He has also released *Messages from The Other Side* a nonfiction book about communication with the dead.

For further information, on his writing, visit G.W. Mullins' web site at ***http://gwmullins.wix.com/books***.

Dream Walker Book One

**Rise Of The Dark-Lighter Book One
Dark Awakening
Is Available in Hardback** (978-1-64871-256-2)**,
Paperback** (978-1-64871-159-6) **and various eBook
formats worldwide.**

Dream Walker Book One

Nuestra Señora de la Santa Muerte, also known as Santa Muerte, is an idol, female deity or folk saint in Mexican and Mexican-American Catholicism. The personification of death, she is believed to be associated with healing, protection, and delivering her devotees safely into the afterlife. Many consider her an angel of death.

Before

The lightning struck around them, as Malachi struggled to steer the car through the debris that the storm threw in their way. His heart raced and he could feel the pounding in his chest. He was scared, probably more scared than he had ever been before. For once in his self-absorbed life, this was not about him, a life was on the line.

"Hang on Uncle, I am doing my best to get us to the hospital. The storm is not making this easy." Malachi tried to comfort him.

"I know, I am holding on. You know I never said how proud I am of you." Carl's voice trailed off into a cough.

"Be still Uncle. There will be time for that after I get you to the hospital."

As Malachi spoke, he attempted to wipe the condensation from the windshield of the car. His efforts were in vain, as he would finish wiping, the fogginess would return. The car was old and barely drivable, it should not have been on the road, but in this situation, he had no choice.

As Malachi looked away to slap his hand against the defroster, he took his eyes off the road. It was then the storm took its vengeance and a funnel cloud passed in front of them. As its winds ripped through the road, a huge oak tree began to sway. Malachi looked up just in time to see it uprooted and flying towards the car.

Malachi let out a scream, as he knew there was nothing he could do to get out of the tree's path. As the tree hit the front grill of the car, it spun out of control and rolled down the deserted street. Flipping end over end, the crushed vehicle landed at the white picket fence that surrounded a country church.

As he looked out through the broken windshield, Malachi felt the blood running down his forehead. Struggling to lift his arm to his head, he felt the pain of being thrown around the vehicle in the crash. He was not sure, but the pain in his chest felt like a cracked rib. The pain came in jabs with his every movement. At first, he did not think of his uncle, then the realization hit him, he was not hearing any noise from the back seat.

Malachi turned to look around. A feeling of dread washed over him. How could his uncle have survived? The man was at death's door before the crash. Looking to the backseat, there was nothing. He was alone in the car.

Looking up through the broken glass, he scanned the road, until he found the form of a body laying several feet behind. His heart sank as he assumed the worst. He had failed with is most important thing he had ever had to do. Pushing against the seat, Malachi attempted to move his battered body to the driver's side door. He pulled the handle and leaned in, but the door was bent and mangled.

Leaning back, Malachi pulled his legs to his chest. He felt the surge of pain as he tried to hold them back with his arms. With all the energy he could muster, he let loose and kicked the door. It flew open quickly, and with such a force, that it slammed into the fender and then to the ground.

Malachi crawled out of the opening and fell to his knees. His head spun around, as dizziness overtook him. The rain blasted all around, as he tried to look towards his uncle. With every drop that hit his head, the blood that covered him splattered and ran down his face. It was no time, before his entire face was covered in red. His eyes stung and burned as he tried to focus, and began to try to get to his feet.

He wobbled back and forth, and lost his footing, falling to the ground as soon as he stood up. He was determined. His mind raced and his life flashed before him. He had accomplished nothing in the twenty years he had been alive. His past was a blur of selfishness and a desire to acquire money.

As he slammed into the paved road, his parent's faces ran through his mind. He wondered if they would have been ashamed of him. He never considered it before. They died when he was very young. He barely knew them. It was then his uncle Carl came and took him in. Malachi felt tears welling in his burning eyes, as he realized the only person on earth that cared for him, was just a few feet away and dying.

Malachi pushed his hands onto the pavement and forced himself upwards. Crawling at first, he finally got his footing and made his way to the lifeless body he saw before him. He fell to his knees at Carl's side and screamed out.

"Be still young one, I am not dead yet." A quiet shaky voice came from Carl's lips.

"Uncle, you are alive. I thought you were…"

"Dead…you can say the word. We all must die sometime, just not this minute. Perhaps soon though." Carl began to cough with his last words.

"No, I will get you help. I promise you I will."

"Malachi, just calm yourself. Go to the church and see if anyone is there. If the priest is in, get him to come and bring me inside."

Malachi rose to his feet, and moved as quickly as he could, to the church doors. As he pulled at the handles, the doors did not move. They were locked. Malachi knew he had to find a way to get his uncle out of the storm. He drew back his fists and threw them at the red wooden door. He screamed out, as he beat on the wood, and threw himself against it trying to force his way in. Just as he was about to give up, the door opened.

"What is happening here?" Father Timothy said hastily as he looked down and saw the bloody face of Malachi. "What has happened to you my boy?"

"The storm, it caused the car to crash and my uncle is badly hurt."

"Why would you come out in a mess like this anyway?" The priest asked.

"My uncle was ill before we left, I think he is dying. Please, can you help him?"

The two made their way to Carl, who was passing in and out of consciousness. Father Timothy took hold of him, and Malachi assisted as they lifted Carl from the ground. The rain pounded down heavily upon them, as they made their way to the door of the church.

Safely inside, they laid Carl's limp body on a pew, near the front of the chapel. Carl's lips moved as if he was speaking to someone. Malachi was not sure of who, he was not sure he wanted to know. He was only sure he was more scared than he had ever been. He looked down at his hands, as they shook uncontrollably. He tried not to succumb to his fears.

The priest returned with towels and a cup of hot tea. As he reached down to Malachi, the boy just looked up to him, barely able to form words. Taking the drink, Malachi held it in his hands, warming them as the priest began to wipe the blood from his forehead and face. Malachi smiled at him trying to find the strength to say thank-you.

"Your uncle needs help that I cannot provide. I can take care of the spiritual end, but honestly, that will not save him. He needs a doctor and medicine. From the looks of him, he was having a heart attack, long before you came out into the storm." Father Timothy said as he continued to clean Malachi's wounds.

"How do we get a doctor? The storm is worse than before. I cannot go anywhere without a car." The boy said, as he hung his head.

"You cannot go anywhere regardless, you are injured. The storm is no place for you in your condition. I will go. I know the roads, and a few shortcuts."

"But how will you get there? You can't walk in this storm."

"I have a motorcycle. It was donated to the church years ago. and I have become very good at riding it. Don't look at me like that, I might be a priest, but I can do normal things you know. Stay here and watch over your uncle. I will be back as soon as I can."

"Father, please be careful. Oh, and thank-you for what you are about to do."

Timothy acknowledged him, and turned to go. Malachi admired his bravery. He wished he was braver than he was. He returned to his uncle's side looking down at him. Carl was still moving his mouth as if he were speaking. The words were not intelligible, but still he spoke under his breath.

As Malachi watched, his uncle's eyes flew open and he pulled his arms close to his chest. Calling out, his voice began to make sense, and his words were clearer. He looked to Malachi and stretched out an arm to grab at him.

Malachi went down on his knees and took his uncle's hand. "What is it uncle. Are you feeling better?"

"No, my boy, I am fighting. The demons of death are coming for me. I need help to fight them. I need you to pray for me. Pray to Santa Muerte, ask her to help me. She will come."

"Uncle, she is not real, she is only a myth. Old Spanish women prey to her as a way to escape their unhappiness." Malachi insisted.

"She is not a myth, she is real. I have known many who have seen her, she comes when life is about to end. She can save me. Please do this for me. You must give her an offering. Place a bowl of water at the alter and pray to her."

"I do not believe in this or in religion, but if it will calm you, I will do it. Now rest as I go find water."

As Malachi searched through the building, he found the kitchen and a bowl for the water. As he filled it, he shook his head, not believing he was about to participate in this craziness. In his heart he knew he had to do it, if for no other reason, to calm his uncle until help came.

Malachi returned to the chapel and placed the water near a statue and cross, in the front of the room. As he kneeled on the floor, he looked up at the Virgin Mary. He wished he believed, in this religion, or in anything that would help them. His heart was too cold and barren he thought.

As he bowed his head, he began to ask for help from Santa Muerte. He asked her to come to him, to aid him in the saving of his uncle. He offered her the bowl of water as an act of respect. Then he closed his eyes. He called for help, and the darkness answered back.

The light in the room faded, as a shadow came forward from the darkened back wall. The figure of a woman took shape. She had dark features and her head was bowed. As she slowly walked forward, Malachi looked up. He prepared to scream, as she raised a shriveled finger to her dried lips.

As he looked at her, he could make out her face, it was drawn and looked as if she had been dead. She retained the features of a woman, but was as much skeleton as human. Her skin looked as if it had been wrapped around bone with no real meat left to her body. Malachi was scared, and his heart raced as she slowly moved towards him.

As she came in his direction, Malachi fell backwards from the feet of the statue. He scrambled trying to get upright. A scream became trapped in his lips as he crawled to the side of his uncle.

Leaning down, Santa Muerte picked up the bowl of water. She moved it to her leathery looking lips and allowed the water to pass into her mouth. She drank until the water was gone. Then she sat the bowl back down and turned towards them.

Malachi stared at her, as she began to smile. As he looked, her appearance began to change. With every second, she became more human in appearance. Her skeletal structure became more flesh-like. Her body filled out, and her face became normal. She laughed out-loud as the transformation became complete.

"Your offering is accepted. I needed that. But why have you disturbed my sleep. It has been many years since I graced this plane. No one has called out to me in over a decade." Santa Muerte looked at him inquisitively.

"My uncle, he is ill. I fear he is dying. Please save him." Malachi pleaded with her.

Extending a hand, she reached down and touched Carl's head. She smiled at him as Carl looked back to her. A joy rushed over him as he saw that Malachi had done as he asked. Carl sat up as Santa Muerte cradled him in her arms.

"Your time to leave this plane was not meant to be as of yet." She spoke softly.

"What do you mean? Is he not dying?"

"That is not what I meant. He was not supposed to die for some time yet. His fate has changed."

"Can you save him?" Malachi pleaded for answers.

"It does not work that way ignorant boy. Life cannot just be given. It is an exchange. A life for a life. One forfeits, so another may live. For him to continue in this existence, another must take his place in death. Now that wouldn't be fair, would it boy?" She asked him.

"No, but I do not want him to die. You have to save him."

"Not everything is by your human choosing. If he is to live, then you tell me whose life to claim in his place. Would you choose that I take the life of the priest that left here unselfishly trying to save another, or perhaps another innocent who does not even know you. Or perhaps, you are willing to exchange your life for his?" She laughed out hysterically, as she walked around looking at the statues in the church.

"No, this cannot be. Malachi, do not even consider her offer. If this is the only way, then I choose death. Take me now Angel of Death. I believed in you and what you stand for. I had no idea you were so cruel and heartless." Carl screamed at her.

"Heartless," she laughed. "I am here to save you, and you call me heartless. I should strike you down myself for your disrespect. I was human like you, and I know the pain of death. You lived much longer than I did. Do not whine to me about your pathetic life. If you want to live, a choice must be made."

"Is there no other way?" Malachi pleaded with her.

"Perhaps, there is. I tire of coming here to this existence to take lives. Become my apprentice, help in my work. Then in the time of one year, you can win back your freedom, if you fulfill your duties."

"You mean, I would not die, and I can come back to my life."

"As pathetic as it is. Yes, you can return, but only at a time I agree. Your Uncle will live, and may do so until his actual time of death that was ordained."

"Then I agree to your terms." Malachi choked on his words.

"No, Malachi do not let her take you. She will not honor the deal. Run from here." Carl screamed.

"It is too late old man, I have him now. The deal is struck. He is mine."

As she turned to look back at Carl, she reached out a hand and Malachi took it. As they walked towards the back hall of the church, they both faded into darkness. Carl stood up, feeling the energy flowing through him again. He was healed, and his life returned. Malachi was not so lucky.

Chapter 1 - Out of The Past

Santa Muerte stood looking, through her portal into the past. She thought about her new apprentice. She watched as he slept. Her mind raced to when she was still human. Moving her hand over the portal, she saw the mist change within, the images went back to the time of 1847. The Mexican-American war raged through Texas. She stared on until she saw herself.

She clung to her mother, as they made their way through the side street trying to avoid the spray of bullets. Her mother pulled her close. Fear covered her face; she had no idea how to save them. They were surrounded by the fighting.

As her mother pulled her into the shelter at the end of the house, Anna looked up to her. She did not understand what was happening. Her mother clung to her trying to quiet her cries.

"Anna…" Her mother spoke. Santa Muerte played the moment over and over again. It had been so long since she had heard her own name said, or her mother's voice saying it. Her cold heart throbbed in her chest. She wasn't supposed to feel this way anymore. She had given up feeling anything about life or people years ago. It was too much of a toll on her. When she inherited her role as an angel of death, she left so much behind.

Looking back into the past, she watched her mother as she cared for Anna who was only six. This war was no place for her. Children were supposed to be carefree and happy. She should have been playing somewhere in a field of flowers. Instead, she was facing an army of soldiers. Santa Muerte glanced down for a moment, she knew what was coming, and that much could still hurt her.

"Mi amor, I promise this is not what I planned for you in life. Please, no matter what happens, remember mama loved you so much. If I could have changed this, I would have. I just do not know how to save you or myself."

As Carlotta finished speaking, she heard the soldiers making their way down the side street. She pulled Anna close and covered her mouth. "Do not cry, do not make a sound." She whispered, as the door began to open slowly. Carlotta raised her head as she came eye to eye with the enemy she had come to fear.

"Stand up woman." He screamed at her.

"Please, I beg of you, spare my child." She cried out.

As the soldier studied her, he did not care for her or her child. He raised his rifle into the air. A smile crossed his lips, as he prepared to claim another notch for his collection of kills. The shot rang out, as Anna watched her mother fall sideways on the ground.

Anna screamed and grabbed at her mother. She pulled at Carlotta's hand, but she did not move.

Anna struggled to arouse her mother, it was no use, she was gone. The young girl had no concept of death or murder. In that day, she witnessed both within minutes. She stood looking at her mother and screaming, as the soldier reloaded his rifle.

"Looks like my lucky day, two Mexicans at the same time. Don't worry, it will be over soon." He said laughing at Anna.

She stood there watching, paralyzed by her own fear. Santa Muerte yelled at her, "Why don't you run and hide. Just save yourself." She raised her hands to her head, as the sound of the rifle firing, rang through the room. Clutching her chest, she caressed the point where the bullet had hit her. If she still had a heart, she thought it would hurt.

Her eyes filled with tears as she watched. The soldier left, walking away proud of himself and his deeds. She felt hatred filling her. She grinned, and thought to herself, there must still be some emotions left inside somewhere. As the killer turned to leave the alley, a Mexican soldier came from around the corner and fired before he was seen. The murderer fell to the ground, a grim look on his face. As he looked up, he saw the dark one coming for him.

A few feet away, the dark shadow came. As it moved forward, it took shape. A man emerged from within the darkness. Dressed in black from head to toe, he wore a dress suit and looked like an undertaker. Looking about, the dark one studied the area. "So many dead, so many souls to claim. I'll be here a while." The Angel of Death was pleased.

He cleared the street of the dead before surveying the area. He made his way down the street until finding the bodies of Carlotta and Anna. Looking down at Anna, he shook his head. "Little One, you never had a chance in life, did you?"

As he lifted Anna into his arms, he carried her through the streets. His pain was obvious, as he struck out at those who caused the death of such a young girl. In moments, he killed all who were in the immediate area, before lifting himself upwards with the child still in his arms.

In his own realm, he took Anna to his private chamber. There he took a small amount of his power and formed a ball of energy in front of him. Looking down at the girl, he aimed his hand, shooting the power within her. "My child, forgive me for what I do, but this is the only way I know to give you life again." With the power surging through her, she took a deep breath, and sat up coughing.

"Arise Muerte. My child, born of death."

"My name is Anna, she said staring at him."

"You were Anna, now you are so much more. You are Queen of the Dead."

"I don't understand." She questioned him.

"In time, it will all make sense to you. But for now, you will grow and learn."

As his words echoed through the room, Malachi watched from behind. He had been watching the whole time. He understood a little

better what was happening. He had enlisted his soul
with that of the dead.

<u>Also Available From G.W. Mullins</u>

Rise Of The Snow Queen Book Two The War Of
The Witches

Daniel Awakens A Ghost Story Begins– From The
Dead Of Night Prequel

Daniel Is Waiting A Ghost Story – From The Dead
Of Night Book One

Daniel Returns A Ghost Story - From The Dead Of
Night Book Two

Daniel's Fate A Ghost Story Ends - From The Dead
Of Night Book Four

Rise Of The Snow Queen Book One The Polar Bear
King

Messages From The Other Side Stories of the Dead,
Their Communication, and Unfinished Business

Vengeance

Mysteries Of The Unseen World – Ghost, Hauntings
and The Unexplained

Dream Walker Book One

Haunted America Stories Of Ghost, Hauntings And The Unexplained

Timeless – A Paranormal Romance Murder Mystery

Star People, Sky Gods, And Other Tales Of The Native American Indians

More Star People, Sky Gods, And Other Paranormal Tales Of The Native American Indians

Lost Tales Of The Native American Indians Vol 1

Walking With Spirits Native American Myths, Legends, And Folklore Volumes One Thru Six

The Native American Cookbook

Native American Cooking - An Indian Cookbook With Legends And Folklore

The Native American Story Book - Stories Of The American Indians For Children
Volumes One Thru Five

The Best Native American Stories For Children

Cherokee A Collection of American Indian Legends, Stories And Fables

Creation Myths - Tales Of The Native American Indians

Strange Tales Of The Native American Indians

Spirit Quest - Stories Of The Native American Indians

Animal Tales Of The Native American Indians

Medicine Man - Shamanism, Natural Healing, Remedies And Stories Of The Native American Indians

Native American Legends: Stories Of The Hopi Indians Volumes One and Two

Totem Animals Of The Native Americans

The Best Native American Myths, Legends And Folklore Volumes One Thru Three

Ghosts, Spirits And The Afterlife In Native American Indian Mythology And Folklore

Dream Walker Book One

War Song: Tales Of The Native American Indians

Origin Tales Of The Native American